"It would be sensible of us to marry."

Benedict leaned back in his chair, gazing over the desk with his usual calm friendliness. "I need a wife, Sibella needs a mother. We will leave the romance out of it for the time being. I think I am right in believing you've had your fill of falling in love?"

Prudence said hesitantly, "And suppose we don't ever — that is, if we just remain on a friendly basis?"

"Shall we cross that bridge when we come to it? You fit into our lives so well, Prudence. I believe we could lead a contented life, you and I and Sibella."

She didn't look at him. She was too busy pondering the strangeness of his proposal. *Contentment.* Was that all he wanted from her, when she could have given him love?

Books by Betty Neels

HARLEQUIN ROMANCES

These books may be available at your local bookseller.

For a free catalog listing all titles currently available,
send your name and address to:

Harlequin Reader Service
P.O. Box 52040, Phoenix, AZ   85072-2040
Canadian address: Stratford, Ontario N5A 6W2

Never Too Late

Betty Neels

Harlequin Books

TORONTO • NEW YORK • LONDON
AMSTERDAM • PARIS • SYDNEY • HAMBURG
STOCKHOLM • ATHENS • TOKYO • MILAN

Original hardcover edition published in 1983
by Mills & Boon Limited

ISBN 0-373-02626-9

Harlequin Romance first edition June 1984

CHAPTER ONE

THE ancient church of the village of Little Amwell was crowded to its massive Norman door, its pews brimming over with flowery hats, their wearers keeping up a steady murmur of conversation which vied with Mrs Broad, the organist, as she laboured through a selection of suitable wedding music. The groom was already there, and his best man, it lacked only the bride for the ceremony to begin.

She was at the door now; Mrs Broad's sudden burst of chords sent every head over its shoulder as she began the short journey down the aisle on her uncle's arm to where her bridegroom was waiting and her father stood ready to marry them. She was a very pretty girl, fair-haired and blue-eyed and slim, a vision in white silk and lace, followed by four very small bridesmaids, enchanting in pale blue with wreaths in their hair, and behind them, shooing them gently along, came the only other bridesmaid, a tall curvy girl with a face as pretty as her sister's, only her hair was a burnished golden red and her eyes green. She was in blue too, a colour in which she didn't look her best, but since the bride had strong views about the unlucky properties of green, she had resigned herself to pale blue silk and a wide-brimmed hat of the same shade. She followed slowly down the aisle, looking demurely ahead of her and still managing to see that old Mrs Forbes from the Grange was wearing a quite astonishing mauve hat, and Lady Byron from the

Manor House was in her everlasting beige. She saw Tony, too, standing on the bride's side, looking devastating in his morning coat; a pity he had refused categorically to be one of the ushers. He was marvellous, of course, but sometimes she wished he wasn't quite so conscious of his dignity. She supposed that once she was married to him, at some not yet decided date, she would have to mend her ways; there were several things for which he had already gently but firmly reproved her.

She came to a halt behind Nancy, took her bouquet and hushed the youngest of the bridesmaids. James was beaming at his bride in a most satisfactory way and her father, while not actually smiling, was looking pleased with himself. And why not? she mused. Nancy had done well for herself; James was something up and coming in the business world and had a rather grand flat in Highgate Village, besides which he was a thoroughly nice young man.

Her father began the service and presently, bored with standing still, the bridesmaids began to play up. It was in the course of preventing one of them from prancing off down the aisle that Prudence became aware of the best man. True, she had known that he was there, conspicuous even. From the back he was a large man, topping James by a good head and with massive shoulders. He turned round now, for the very good reason that the bridesmaid had him by the trouser leg, and Prudence could see his face—nice-looking in a rugged way, with fair hair already sprinkled with grey. He removed the small girl's arms from his leg and handed her back and smiled at Prudence. His eyes were very blue and crinkled nicely at the corners. Not a patch on Tony, of course, but he might be fun to know ... She smiled back, and then composed her features into suitable solemnity as the choir launched itself into 'The voice that breathed o'er Eden', the little boys cast their eyes to heaven in an unlikely piety and the men behind them rolled out their notes in a volume of sound. Prudence, from under her brim, watched Mr Clapp, the butcher, bellowing his way through the hymn; he had a powerful voice, used frequently in his shop to cry the virtues of his meat. She took a quick peep at the best man, although there wasn't much to see; broad shoulders and a ramrod back, and when he turned his head slightly, a high-bridged nose and a firm chin. She looked down at her bouquet. The choir had filled their lungs ready for the last verse, but she wasn't heeding them. Traditionally, the chief bridesmaid and the best man paired off at a wedding; it might do Tony a lot of good if he were to be given a cold—well, cool—shoulder; he was, she suspected, getting too sure of her. She hadn't met the best man yet; he had been abroad, James had told her, and had only arrived in time to see that James got safely to the church. Really she knew nothing at all about him. Married most likely, certainly engaged; it would be fun to find out.

The choir, conscious of a job well done, subsided into their pews and her father began the little homily he must know by heart, for she had heard it at countless weddings at which he had officiated. By turning her head very slowly, she could see her mother, still a pretty woman, wearing a Mother of the Bride's hat, and a slightly smug expression. She caught Prudence's eye and smiled and nodded. Prudence was well aware what her mother was thinking—that she would be the next bride, with Tony standing where James was standing now. She would have liked a quiet wedding, but there would be little chance of that. It would be exactly the same as Nancy's, white silk and chiffon and more little bridesmaids. No plans had been made, of course, but she was quite sure that her mother had it all arranged. That lady had been puzzled and disappointed that Prudence hadn't been the first to marry anyway. She was, after all, the eldest, and she was twenty-seven, with a long-standing engagement behind her, there had seemed no reason why she and Tony shouldn't have married before Nancy and James, but Tony had lightheartedly declared that they had plenty of time, there was no hurry. He had a splendid job with a big firm of architects, a pleasant house on the edge of Little Amwell and the prospect of a trip to New York within the next month or so. 'After I'm back,' he had told Prudence easily. 'After all, you're perfectly content and happy at home, aren't you?'

She had been aware of a faint warning at the back of her mind, so absurd that she had ignored it, and then, in the excitement and bustle of the wedding, forgotten it.

But now it came back to tease her. She was by no means content to sit at home and wait for Tony; there had been no reason at all why she shouldn't have married him months ago and gone to New York with him; somehow, the excitement of marrying him had fizzled out like a kettle going off the boil—and yet surely, after three, almost four years, she should know if she loved him or not? Something, she wasn't sure what, would have to be done.

Her father had finished, Mrs Broad was thumping out the opening lines of 'Oh, perfect love' and the choir had surged to its feet with the congregation hard on its heels. The signing took on a new lease of life; the choir thinking of their dinner, the guests of the champagne and buffet lunch awaiting them in the marquee erected on the roomy lawns surrounding the solid Victorian vicarage. It was a bit of an anticlimax to sit down again while the wedding party trailed into the vestry, and presently out again. There had been the usual kissing and congratulations there, but beyond a rather casual greeting from the best man, Prudence had had no chance to speak to him. She went down the aisle beside him presently, her pretty face and vivid hair drawing a good many admiring glances, none of which came from the best man. Benedict van Vinke—a foreign name. Later, if he was disposed to be friendly, she would ask him where he came from.

But although he was friendly enough, he wasn't disposed to tell her much. He parried her questions with lazy good humour, smiling at her with a flicker of amusement in his eyes. She ended up discovering almost nothing. He was a Dutch doctor, he travelled a good deal, he had known James for a number of years, they had in fact been at Cambridge together. Beyond these snippets of information he didn't go, and presently she wandered off, still wondering about him, to do her duty by the other guests.

Tony joined her presently, and it pleased her to see that he looked annoyed. He gave her a severe look. 'Even if you are chief bridesmaid, there's no need to sit in the best man's pocket. Everyone here knows that we're going to get married and it's hardly the thing for you to spend the entire time with him.'

'Are you jealous, Tony?' she wanted to know.

'Certainly not! Jealousy is a complete waste of good sense, I merely observed that other people might think . . .'

'You mind what they think?' Prudence asked, her green eyes very bright.

'Naturally I mind. The opinion of other people is important to a professional man.'

'And that's the reason you're annoyed with me?' Prudence lowered long dark lashes over her eyes. 'I must go and say hullo to Lady Brinknell.'

She sauntered off, but not to the lady in question. She fetched up again beside Benedict van Vinke, waited patiently until the couple he was talking to wandered away, and asked: 'If you were going to marry a girl and she spent a lot of time with another man, at a function like this one, would you be annoyed?'

He smiled down at her. 'Very.'

'Why?'

His eyes widened. 'Obvious reasons. If she were my girl, she wouldn't be allowed to wander off with any Tom, Dick or Harry around.'

'You'd be jealous?'

'Very.'

'And you wouldn't mind what everyone said? I mean, you wouldn't object just because it might make people gossip?'

'Good lord, no! Who cares what other people think? It's none of their business, anyway.'

Prudence heaved a sigh. 'Oh, well—thank you . . .' She glanced without knowing it in Tony's direction, and Benedict van Vinke said kindly: 'You mustn't take him too seriously, you know.'

She said sharply: 'I don't know what you mean! It was a purely hypothetical question.'

He only smiled and asked lazily: 'When are you going to marry?'

She said crossly: 'I have no idea—and anyway, it's none of your business,' and then, quite forgetting to be annoyed, added wistfully: 'We've been engaged for years and years . . .'

He ignored the last bit. 'No, it isn't,' he agreed equably, 'but after all, it was you who brought the subject up in the first place.'

She was on the point of turning away when Tony joined them. He put a proprietorial arm on Prudence's shoulder. 'May I suggest,' he began, and she wished that he wouldn't preface so many of his wishes with that remark—'that you circulate, Prudence. Lady Byron remarked to me only a few minutes ago that she'd barely set eyes on you, and the Forbeses—people at the Manor, you know,' he explained kindly to Benedict,' were asking to meet you.'

His voice implied that this was an honour indeed, but the large man standing before him, looking at him with a tolerant good humour which set his teeth on edge, only smiled at him. 'I'll be delighted to meet them later on,' he conceded. 'I've a number of old friends to chat with first.'

He made no effort to move away; after a small silence Tony took Prudence's elbow and walked her off. 'It's fortunate that van Vinke is unlikely to see much of us,' he observed frostily. 'I dislike that type of man.'

'What type is he?' asked Prudence; she had her own ideas on that, but it would be interesting to hear Tony's opinion.

'Arrogant, conceited, not bothering to make himself

agreeable. I suggest that you avoid him for the rest of the day, Prudence—besides, he's a foreigner.'

She was struck dumb by the appalling thought that over the years she had allowed herself to be dictated to by Tony. After all, they weren't married yet; he had no right to expect her to conform to his ideas. She said baldly: 'I like him.' She picked up a glass of champagne from the buffet table they were passing, tossed it off, shook his hand from her arm and joined a group of aunts and uncles she barely knew except for the exchange of Christmas cards each year. The champagne, coupled with her indignant feelings, gave her unwonted vivacity, so that her elderly relatives, watching her as she left them presently, remarked among themselves that dear Prudence seemed to have changed a good deal. 'Of course, she is twenty-seven,' observed the most elderly aunt, and pursed her lips and nodded her head wisely, as though twenty-seven was a dangerous age when anything might happen.

The reception, following a time-honoured pattern, drew to its end. The bride and bridegroom disappeared, to reappear shortly in tweed outfits suitable for their honeymoon in Scotland. It was still late August and warm, but Little Amwell, buried in the heart of Somerset, was undoubtedly milder in climate than the far north where Nancy had decided they should go. When Prudence had asked her why, she had said simply: 'It sounds romantic.'

Prudence, handing out bags of confetti among the guests, remembered that remark. Only that morning when Tony had called in on his way to the church, he had made some measured remark about combining business with pleasure when he and Prudence went on honeymoon. There were clients in Hamburg and Oslo who were considering giving his firm a big contract—as he had said, time enough to talk about that when he got back from America; she was content enough at home. Suddenly she knew that she wasn't.

The guests went away slowly, stopping to chat, mull over the wedding and discuss each other's appearance. When the last one had gone, Prudence kicked off her slippers, flung her hat on to a chair and went to the kitchen to give Mabel, grown old in her parents' service, a hand with the tea-tray.

With it in her hands, she kicked open the creaking baize door leading to the front hall and paused to say over her shoulder: 'I'll be back presently, Mabel, and we'll think about supper. Did you enjoy the wedding?'

'A fair treat, Miss Prudence, but you'll look just as pretty when your turn comes.'

Crossing the hall, Prudence had the strange feeling that Mabel's words sounded like a death sentence.

Her parents were in the drawing room. Not alone, for old Aunt Rachel, who lived miles away in Essex, was to stay for a day or two before going home by train. And Tony was there, stretched out in one of the comfortable rather shabby armchairs, looking, thought Prudence crossly, as though he owned the place. To make matters worse, he looked up and grinned at her as she went in, without bothering to get up and take the tray from her. Was he so sure of her already? She dumped it on the sofa table near her mother's chair and sat down, a slow build-up of ill-usage creeping over her. Furthermore, her teeth were set on edge by his careless, 'Tired, old girl?'

She was not his old girl, she argued silently, she was his fiancée, to be cherished and spoilt a little, and certainly not to be taken for granted.

She said haughtily: 'Not in the least,' and addressed herself to Aunt Rachel for almost all of the time they took over tea. And when the elegant little meal was finished, she picked up the tray once more, observing that Mabel needed a hand in the kitchen and adding in a decidedly acidulated tone: 'And perhaps you would open the door, Tony?'

She dumped the tray on the kitchen table and then went to the stove, where she clashed saucepan lids quite unnecessarily until Mabel looked up from the beans she was stringing.

'Now, now! Hoity-toity!' said Mabel.

Prudence didn't answer; she had heard Mabel say just that whenever she or Nancy had displayed ill humour since early childhood, for Mabel had joined the Trent household when Mrs Trent had married and had taken upon herself the role of nanny over and above her other duties, and since Mrs Trent was still, at that time, struggling to be the perfect vicar's wife, Mabel had taken a large share in their upbringing, a process helped along by a number of old-fashioned remarks such as 'Little pitchers have long ears,' and 'Little girls should be seen and not heard,' and 'Keep little fingers from picking and stealing.'

And when Prudence didn't answer, Mabel said comfortably: 'Well, tell old Mabel, then.'

'I don't think I want to get married,' observed Prudence in a ruminating voice.

'And what will your dear ma and pa say to that?'

'I haven't told them—you see, I've only just thought about it in the last hour or so.'

'The wedding's unsettled you, love—seeing our Nancy getting married—girls always have last-minute doubts, so I'm told. Not that you ought to have with such a nice long engagement. They do say, "Marry in haste . . ."'

'Repent at leisure. I know—but, Mabel, Tony and I have been engaged for so long there doesn't seem to be anything left. I think if I married him I'd regret it to my dying day. I want to stay single and do what I want to do for a change, not sit here at home, doing the church flowers and helping with the Mothers' Union on Thursdays and waiting for Tony to decide when we're to be married. I want a career . . .'

'What at?' Mabel's voice was dry.

'Well, I can type, can't I? And do a little shorthand and I've kept the parish accounts for Father for years. I could work in an office.'

'Where?' Mabel put the bowl of beans on the table and went to the sink to wash her hands.

'How should I know? London, I suppose.'

'You wouldn't like that. You listen to me, love. You go back to the drawing room and talk to your Tony, he's a steady young man, making his way in the world.'

'Oh, pooh!' Prudence started slowly for the door. 'For two pins I'd slip out of the garden door!'

'And what's unsettled you, my lady?' asked Mabel. 'Or is it who?'

But Prudence didn't answer, only the door closed with a snap behind her.

Tony was still there when she got back to the drawing room and he barely paused in what he was saying to her father to nod at her. Prudence went and sat down by her mother and listened to that lady's mulling over of the wedding in company with Aunt Rachel.

'And when is it to be your turn?' asked her aunt.

'I don't know,' said Prudence, then raised her voice sharply. 'Tony—Aunt Rachel wants to know when we're getting married.'

Tony had frowned slightly; he did dislike being interrupted when he was speaking and Prudence's voice had sounded quite shrewish. 'At the moment I have so many commitments that it's impossible to even suggest a date.'

His voice held a note of censure for her and Aunt Rachel asked in surprise: 'But I always thought that the bride chose her wedding date?'

He chose to take the remark seriously, and it struck Prudence, not for the first time, perhaps, that his sense of humour was poor. 'Ah, but I'm really the one to be considered, you see. I have an exacting profession and Prudence, living quietly at home as she does, need only fall in with my wishes, without any disruption of her own life.'

Mrs Trent looked up at that with a look of doubt on her face and even the Reverend Giles Trent, a dreamy man by nature, realised that something wasn't quite as it should be. It was left to Prudence to remark in a deceptively meek voice: 'Nothing must stand in Tony's way now that he's making such a success of his career.'

She looked at them all, her green eyes sparkling, smiling widely, looking as though she had dropped a heavy burden. Which she had—Tony.

She didn't say a word to anyone, least of all Tony, who, the day following the wedding went up to London, explaining rather pompously that there was a good deal of important work for him to do. 'Stuff I can't delegate to anyone else. I shall probably be back at the weekend.' He had dropped a kiss on her cheek and hurried off.

She wasted no time. With only the vaguest ... what she intended to do, she spent every free mo.. of at the typewriter in her father's study, getting up H speed, and after she had gone to bed each evening, she got out pencil and paper and worked hard at her shorthand. She wasn't very good at it, but at least she had a basic knowledge of it, enough perhaps to get by in some office. She began to read the adverts in the *Telegraph*, but most of them seemed to be for high-powered personal assistants with phenomenal speeds. Perhaps she would do better at some other job, only she had no idea what it might be. Nursing had crossed her mind, but she was a bit old to start training—besides, although she had done her St John Ambulance training to set a good example to the village, she had never quite mastered bandaging and finer variations of the pulse had always evaded her. All the same, she didn't lose heart. She welcomed Tony at the weekend when he called after church, and listened to his plans for the trip to New York with becoming attention, while her head was filled with vague hopeful plans for her own future. It was on the tip of her tongue several times to tell him that she had decided that she couldn't marry him after all, but that, she realised, would be silly. She must wait until she had a job—any job that would make her independent. He was so sure of her that he wouldn't believe her; she would need proof to convince him.

August slipped gently into September and Nancy and James came back from their honeymoon to spend a few days at the Vicarage before setting up house in Highgate. It was at the end of this visit that Nancy suggested that Prudence might like to spend a weekend with them. 'James thinks that we ought to

some of his friends who couldn't come to the
wedding, for drinks one evening—it'll be a Saturday,
so why don't you come for a couple of nights? I don't
know many of them and it would be nice if you were
there too. Let's see, it's Thursday—what about
Saturday week? Come up on Friday night so that you
can help me get things ready.'

Prudence hesitated. 'It sounds fun, but won't you
and James want to be alone for a bit?'

'Well, we won't be alone if we have a party, will
we?' Nancy declared. 'And Tony's off to the States
anyway. Say you'll come?'

So it was arranged, and Tony, when he was told,
thought it a very good idea. 'You'll find it dull without
me,' he pointed out. 'Besides, I daresay you'll meet
some people who may be useful later on.' He patted
Prudence rather absentmindedly on the shoulder.
'Never mind, old girl, I'll be back in a couple of
weeks.'

And by then, thought Prudence, I'll have got
myself a job. For a moment she felt a guilty pang,
borne away on a tide of indignation when he said
casually: 'There's a chance I'll have to go to
Portugal in a couple of months; some tycoon wants a
villa designed in the Algarve and he wants someone
over there for consultation. A bit of luck for
me—the weather should be pretty good in
November.' He paused and glanced at her. 'I don't
care for the idea of a winter wedding, do you,
Prudence? And there's no hurry. I'll take a couple of
weeks off in the spring . . .'

'What for?' asked Prudence in a very quiet voice.

'It'll be a convenient time for us to get married. I'll
be able to give you a definite date later on. Though of

course, if anything turns up . . .' He gave a self-satisfied smile. 'I am rather in demand.'

Prudence's eyes glittered greenly. 'Your career means a lot to you, doesn't it, Tony?' she asked.

'Well, of course it does—darling, you do say the stupidest things sometimes! Well, I must be off. You're going to Nancy's next Saturday? I leave on the Monday after that, I'll give you a ring if I can't find time to get to Highgate.'

Prudence drove herself up to London in the secondhand Mini Aunt Rachel had given her for her twenty-first birthday. It was a bit battered by now, but it went well enough, and she was a good driver. The flat in Highgate, the ground floor of an imposing Victorian mansion set in a roomy garden, had welcoming lights shining from its windows as she stopped the little car before its door. Nancy had said, 'Come in good time for dinner,' but Prudence had cut it rather fine, what with having to type her father's sermon at the last minute, and round up the choirboys for an extra choir practice for Harvest Festival.

Nancy was at the door before she had time to ring the bell and dragged her inside. 'Oh, isn't this fun? You're late—I was in a panic that you wouldn't be coming. There's masses of stuff in the kitchen to see to ready for tomorrow evening.'

She hurried Prudence inside and swept her into the sitting room where James was waiting, and for a time the kitchen was forgotten while they sat with their drinks, talking over the honeymoon and the marvels of Highgate and how marvellous it was to nip into Harvey Nichols or Harrods with absolutely no trouble at all. Prudence listened with pleasure to her sister's chatter and presently followed her to the back of the flat, to the pretty room she was to sleep in. 'And when you've dolled yourself up, we'll have dinner and then decide about tomorrow's food,' declared Nancy happily. At the door she paused, looking at Prudence. 'Darling, you really must get married soon—it's such fun!'

To which Prudence, living up to her name for once, made no reply.

They all repaired to the kitchen after dinner. Mrs Turner, the daily housekeeper, had gone home leaving the way clear for them to prepare whatever was needed for the party, and since Nancy was rather a slapdash cook and James did nothing but eat samples of what was laid out on the table, it fell to Prudence's lot to make pastry for the vol-au-vents, choux pastry for the little cream cakes Nancy had decided to offer her guests, and bake the sausage rolls. There was to be far more than these, of course. Nancy reeled off a list of the delicacies she had planned and then perched on the kitchen table watching Prudence.

'You're such a super cook,' she said presently. 'Tony doesn't know how lucky he is.'

Prudence looked up from her mixing bowl. 'I'm not going to marry Tony.' She spoke defiantly.

The two of them stared at her. 'Not marry . . . but why not?'

It was James who said slowly: 'You've been engaged a very long time.'

Prudence nodded. 'Yes, that's partly it—I mean, we've had the chance to marry—oh, ever since we were engaged. It's gone sour . . . Tony doesn't really want me; he wants someone to bolster up his career.'

'What will you do?' She blessed James for being so matter-of-fact about it.

'Get a job. I've been mugging up my shorthand and typing, they're not very good, but I daresay I could manage some sort of office job. I don't want to stay at home.' She added impatiently: 'I'm twenty-seven, you know.'

'There's no reason why you shouldn't find something,' observed James reasonably. 'There are jobs going—receptionists and so on, where even if typing is needed, it's not essential—shorthand is always useful, of course. If I hear of anything I'll let you know.'

'You're an angel,' declared Prudence. 'I can quite see why Nancy married you.' She beamed at him and went back to her cooking.

The party was for half past six so that those who had evening engagements could go on to them and those who hadn't could stay as long as they liked. Prudence, hair and face carefully done, wearing a green dress that matched her eyes, went along to the sitting room in good time to help with the last-minute chores, and when the first of the guests arrived, melted into the background. It was, after all, Nancy's party, and someone was needed to keep an eye on the food and trot to and fro to the kitchen to replenish plates.

It was on one of these trips, while she was piling another batch of vol-au-vents on to plates, that the kitchen door opened and Benedict van Vinke strolled in. His hullo was friendly and casual, and he ignored her surprise. 'Thought I'd drop in for an hour,' he observed mildly, 'and see how James and Nancy are getting on! Nice party—did you make these things?' He ate a couple of vol-au-vents and turned his attention to the tiny sausage rolls she had taken out of the oven.

'Yes, I like cooking. What a lot of friends they've got.' She took off her oven gloves and took a sausage roll and began to eat it.

'Where's Tony?' he asked.

She said carefully: 'I don't know—somewhere in London, I suppose. He's going to the States on Monday. He said he might find time to come over.'

He opened blue eyes wide. 'Surely he allows himself a few hours off at weekends?'

'He's very busy—he's a successful architect, you know.'

'Yes, I did know—he told me.' His voice was dry.

'And what do you do?' asked Prudence snappily, on edge for some reason she couldn't understand.

'I'm a G.P.' He took another sausage roll and picked up the dish. 'I'll carry these in for you.'

She led the way back to the sitting room with a distinct flounce, quite out of temper at his mild snub.

The last of the guests left about nine o'clock, but Benedict didn't go with them; Nancy had invited him to stay for a cold supper later on, and Prudence guessed from his unsurprised acceptance that he was a frequent visitor. Indeed, he seemed to know his way about the place just as well as his host and hostess, laying the small round table in the dining room and going down to the cellar to bring up the wine while James carved a chicken.

They were half way through the meal when Nancy asked: 'Did you really mean that, Prudence? I mean about not marrying Tony and getting a job?'

Prudence shot a look across the table to Benedict, whose calm face showed no interest whatever. 'Yes, of course I did,' and then she tried a red herring: 'What a success your party was!'

'Yes, wasn't it? Does Tony know?'

'No. I'll—I'll tell him when I see him . . .' She was interrupted by the telephone, and when James came back from answering it, he said cheerfully:

'Well, you'll be able to do that almost at once—that was Tony saying he can spare us half an hour. He's on his way.'

'No,' said Prudence instantly, 'I can't—how can I? I haven't got a job—he'll never believe me unless I can prove that I've found work—I mean, that'll make him see that I mean it.' She stared round at them all. 'I expect I sound like a heartless fool, but I'm not—I've felt—I feel like some Victorian miss meekly waiting for the superior male to condescend to marry me.' She added strongly: 'And I won't!'

'No, of course not,' said James soothingly. 'No one will make you do something you don't want to do— but it's a good opportunity to tell him.' He thought for a minute. 'If he's off to the States it'll make the break much easier—telling people, you know"

Prudence tossed off her wine, choked, spluttered and said between whoops: 'Could I tell a fib and say I'd found a job, do you think?'

For the first time Benedict spoke. 'That would hardly become a parson's daughter,' he observed mildly, 'and perhaps there's no need. It just so happens that I'm badly in need of a general factotum— someone to type—you do type, I hope? My English letters, make sure that I keep appointments, do the flowers, keep an eye on the household and my small daughter. Not much of a job, I'm afraid, but a very necessary one.'

Prudence had her eyes on her face. She said slowly: 'You're married?'

He smiled a little. 'A widower—Sibella is six years old. I live in an old-fashioned rambling house which I am told is sheer hell to cope with, in Appeldoorn.'

'Holland?' queried Prudence.

'That's right,' he answered her seriously, although his eyes were dancing. 'Although I spend a good deal of time over here. You could start at once or within a few days, just as you wish.' And as the doorbell rang, 'You'll have to decide here and now; that sounds like Tony.'

Nancy had gone to open the door and Tony followed her into the room. His eyes swept the rather untidy table and came to rest on Prudence. 'I see you're enjoying yourself, Prudence,' he remarked, and nodded to James and Benedict. 'Lucky little girl, aren't you, while I spend my days hard at work!'

She didn't answer him, she looked across the table at Benedict. She said very clearly: 'Yes.' Being called a little girl had been the last straw; she stood five feet seven in her stockings and she was a big girl.

James broke the silence with some remark about Tony's trip and they listened to his pompous reply before Nancy asked: 'Will you have a drink, Tony? Or I'll make some fresh coffee. James and Benedict were just going to wash up in the kitchen—I expect you two would like to be alone for a bit.'

Prudence cast her sister a telling glance, but before she could answer Tony said: 'As to that, I don't give much for these sentimental partings and I won't stay for coffee—there's a man I have to see before I leave . . .'

'I'm not going to marry you,' said Prudence suddenly, and the four of them looked at her, Nancy and James with sympathy Tony with outraged astonishment and Benedict van Vinke with faint amusement.

'Don't talk rubbish!' said Tony sharply.

'It's not rubbish.' Prudence took the ring off her finger and put it on the table. 'We could have been married a dozen times in these last four years, Tony, and now it's too late.'

'You've decided to be a dutiful daughter and live at home?' he asked with a faint sneer.

'No, I've got a job.'

'You've never done a day's work in your life—what can you do?'

'Prudence has agreed to join my household as a personal assistant to me and companion to my small daughter.' Benedict's voice was quiet, but there was a hint of steel in it which made Tony pause before he answered.

He said stiffly: 'We don't need anyone interfering in our affairs. I'll talk to Prudence.' He turned to her. 'Come into another room and we'll settle this once and for all.'

'No need—it's settled. I'm sorry, Tony, but I'm not the right wife for you—you must know that, because if I had been, you'd have married me years ago.' She picked up the ring. 'Here you are. I hope you have a successful trip.'

She went out of the room rather quickly and went into the kitchen and shut the door. Even though she knew she had done the right thing, it was a little frightening to find herself alone after almost four years, and now she had committed herself to a job she knew nothing about in a country she had never been to with a man she had met only for the second time that evening. She felt lightheaded with relief and regret for what might have been, and at the same time scared of the future.

CHAPTER TWO

PRUDENCE was vaguely aware of voices, the faint thump of the front door closing and a moment later the door behind her opening.

'Tea?' Benedict's voice sounded matter-of-fact as he crossed to the sink, filled the kettle and set it to boil. He didn't look at her as he went on: 'Your habit of drinking tea at all times is one to which I strongly subscribe.'

'You're Dutch?' Prudence hadn't given it a thought until now. 'Why is your English so good?'

'Perhaps because I spend a good deal of time in England. I went to school here and then Cambridge, but I am still a Dutchman, through and through.'

'I don't know a thing about you.' And then because she couldn't help herself: 'Has he gone?'

'Yes.' He gave her a lightning glance and poured water into a teapot. 'There's not much to tell—I'm a G.P. My home is in Appeldoorn, a rather pleasant town in the centre of Holland—I've already told you that, haven't I?' He found a mug and filled it to the brim. 'Drink that—we won't talk any more about it tonight, you're not registering anyway. I'll come round tomorrow morning and we'll go for a walk and discuss your duties.' And when she looked at him in a puzzled way: 'You agreed to come and work for me.'

'Yes—yes, and I meant it, that is if you think I could cope?'

'Why shouldn't you cope?' he wanted to know coolly. 'There's almost no skill involved.'

Prudence frowned. 'That sounds rude.'

'It's not meant to be—what I mean is that it's a job that any sensible woman could do, and you seem sensible.'

'Oh—do I? Well, I can type and do a shaky shorthand and I can cook and keep house and do simple accounts, and I've taught in Sunday School for ten years.'

'Exactly the kind of person I'm looking for.' He smiled at her and opened the kitchen door. 'Let's join the others.'

Nancy and James didn't say anything; they were making rather a thing of clearing up, and it wasn't until Benedict began a lighthearted conversation about the party that they joined in, looking relieved. Benedict went shortly after that with the casual remark that he would be along about ten o'clock the next morning; he wished Nancy and James goodbye, then stopped in front of Prudence. 'We all get our bad moments,' he told her kindly. 'They don't last, if that's any consolation to you, though they're the very devil while they're there.'

He squeezed her shoulder with an enormous hand and she felt strangely comforted.

She hadn't expected to sleep, but she did, and woke feeling such relief that everything was all over and done with that it quite washed out any other feeling. Nancy and James, prepared to treat her with cautious sympathy, were surprised to see her eat a good breakfast and listen to her cheerful comments about the party. 'And you don't have to worry about me,' she assured them. 'I ought to have done it ages ago— I'm sure that Tony's as relieved as I am—he'll find himself an American heiress, I've no doubt.' She looked at her sister. 'Was he very upset when he went?' Her voice faltered a little. 'I should have stayed, but I just couldn't.'

'Of course you couldn't,' said Nancy warmly. 'If you mean was he unhappy about it—no, I don't think he was; his pride had had a nasty jolt and he was worried about people talking. Are you really going to work for Benedict?'

'Oh, yes, it sounds the kind of job I can manage without falling flat on my face, he said he'd tell me about it when he comes this morning.'

'He'd better stay to lunch,' said Nancy.

Benedict arrived at ten o'clock, declined coffee, enquired if Prudence was ready and when she had got a jacket to cover her jersey dress, walked her briskly to Highgate Ponds, across Parliament Hill and so on to Hampstead Heath. He didn't talk about anything much until they were turning back in the direction of Highgate Ponds once more, and as for Prudence, she was happy to walk and enjoy her surroundings and not think too much.

They had been silent in a comfortable companionship way for a minute or two when he asked to surprise her: 'Do you have any money of your own?'

She stared at him in surprise. 'Me? Yes, a small income from some money my godmother left me. Why?'

'It makes it so much easier,' he explained. 'If you don't like the job you won't feel that you must stay because you need the money.'

'I hadn't thought of that. But I'm sure I'll like it; I do want to do something, not just stay at home. Mother and Father don't actually need me there, in fact Mother has been hinting for months that it would be nice when Tony and I got married.'

He made no comment, but asked: 'You're sure it is what you want? It's not in the least exciting and there will be no regular hours—though I'll see that you get a day to yourself each week. Bring your car over if you like so that you can get around.'

'Thank you. I can't speak a word of Dutch.'

'You'll soon pick it up,' he dismissed that airily, 'and you'll be dealing with my English correspondence.'

'Yes, but does your little girl speak English?'

'After a fashion. I'd be glad if you'd speak nothing but your own language with her.'

'And what else would you want me to do?'

'Be a Girl Friday, or if that's too frivolous for you, a Universal Aunt.'

Prudence frowned; she might be removed from her first youth, but she felt that she was hardly eligible to be something as staid as a Universal Aunt. 'I think a household assistant sounds better,' she observed coldly.

'Whatever you like,' agreed Benedict suavely, 'but I shall continue to call you Prudence.'

'Shall I have to call you Dr van Vinke?'

'I think it might be a good idea if you're taking letters or if there are patients present, don't you?'

They were almost back at the flat and he slowed his steps. 'Would you like me to come down and see your parents? They don't know me, only as James' friend . . .'

'That would be kind if you can spare the time.'

'I'll give you a ring. Now as to salary—how about seventy pounds a week—or the equivalent in gulden?'

'That's far too much!' Prudence was quite shocked.

'Wait until you've worked for a couple of weeks

before you say that,' he counselled. 'I shall expect value for my money.'

She wasn't sure if she liked that. She said stiffly: 'I shall do my best.'

And that seemed to be the end of it, for the time being at least. Over lunch he and James argued goodnaturedly as to the best route for her to take and before he went he remarked casually that he would let her know more when he next saw her at Little Amwell. His goodbye was casual in the extreme.

He arrived at Little Amwell four days later, which gave Prudence time to tell her parents what she intended doing and allowed them to recover from the shock, although she rather suspected that they weren't unduly upset about her broken engagement. It was, of course, a little awkward having to tell people, but luckily in a village the size of Little Amwell news travelled fast if not always with accuracy. Mabel was told as befitted an old friend, but it wasn't until Mrs Pett, who ran the general stores and Post Office, made a coy reference to Tony's absence that Prudence observed flatly that she was no longer engaged and was on the point of taking a job. Mrs Pett's rather bulbous eyes almost popped from her head. 'My dear soul—and after all this long time, too!'

'Almost four years,' Prudence reminded her, and looked pointedly at the list of groceries she had to buy. 'I'd better have tasty cheese, Mrs Pett,'—she only sold two kinds, tasty and mild, 'I should think half a pound would do.'

Mrs Pett dealt with the cheese. 'So you're going away, Miss Prudence—you'll be missed.'

'Thank you, Mrs Pett.' Prudence wasn't going to be drawn into details; no doubt Mrs Pett would invent those when she passed on the news. She finished her shopping and went back home and spent the rest of the morning going through her wardrobe, deciding what she should take with her. She must remember to ask Benedict what the weather was like in Holland and should she take winter clothes as well or would she be able to come home and collect them later, if she stayed. She might not be suitable—his small daughter might not like her, her shorthand might not stand up to dictation. She had the sneaking feeling that Benedict, placid and friendly as he was, might present quite a different aspect once he got back to his own home and took up a busy routine again. It was a sobering thought, and she spent most of the next day taking down imaginary letters and typing them back not always as successfully as she could wish. Still, she told herself, if she was to look after the little girl and help around the house, there wouldn't be all that time to do his correspondence, and anyway, he couldn't have all that much in English. The thought cheered her so that she flung her notebook down and took Podge the elderly spaniel for an extra long walk.

When she got home there was an Aston Martin Volante outside the front door, dark blue, elegant and powerful. She and Podge circled it slowly before she went indoors, admiring it. 'Very expensive,' said Prudence to the dog, 'and fast—it must drink petrol like I drink tea!'

In the sitting room her mother and father were entertaining Benedict, but they stopped talking as she went in. She greeted him unselfconsciously, adding: 'What a nice car you've got—I didn't know that you had one over here.'

'James drove me down for the wedding and I don't always use it in London. It gets me around, though.'

'So I should imagine.' Prudence looked at her mother. 'I'll help Mabel with tea, shall I?' She turned to Benedict. 'Are you staying the night?'

'Your mother kindly suggested it, but I can't—I'm on my way to Bristol. But tea would be delightful.' He smiled as he spoke and she remembered the last time they had had tea together and went a little pink.

'I'll get it,' she said to no one in particular.

Over tea Benedict enlarged upon her duties, more for the benefit of her parents than herself, she suspected; he also detailed her journey. 'I'm going home in a couple of days' time, perhaps you could follow—let's see—would Friday suit you? That gets you to Appeldoorn on Saturday, which will give you the weekend in which to find your way around and get to know Sitske, my housekeeper—her husband's the gardener and odd job man. I believe they're known as married couples over here—and of course Sibella, she knows you're coming to live with us, but I warn you she's quite a handful. I spend as much time with her as I can, but not as much as I should like. I'm sure you'll fill a much-needed gap for her.'

'Prudence has a way with children,' declared Mrs Trent comfortably. 'If she can keep the Sunday School class in order she can certainly cope with one little girl. I think—we both think—that it will be very nice for Prudence to go away for a while and earn her living—it's quiet here; that didn't matter when she expected to marry, but now it's a chance for her to be independent. How providential that you happened to need someone, Benedict.'

He agreed gravely. 'And how fortunate that I have found Prudence.'

He got up to go presently, bidding them quiet

goodbyes, adding that he would see Prudence on the following Saturday.

She went with him to the door, where he paused for a moment. 'I'll see you get your tickets in good time,' he promised, and before she could say anything, had got into the Aston Martin and zoomed away.

Prudence watched the car turn out of the short drive and go down the village street. She was a good driver herself; she thoroughly approved of the lack of fuss with which he had handled the big car. Tony, she remembered, could never just get in and drive off; things had to be adjusted, knobs turned, lights tested, windows wound up or down, she hadn't realised until now how that had irritated her. She thought that on the whole she was going to like working for Benedict. Of course, she didn't know him; he might be a tyrant in his own home, although she didn't think so.

She wandered back to the sitting room, wishing vaguely that he had told her more about himself, for in fact he had told her very little. He was a widower, she knew that, and she wondered how long he had been without a wife. Perhaps he had told her father. She found the chance to ask him during the evening, and for some reason felt relief when she heard that his wife had died soon after his daughter was born. 'Very sad,' observed her father, and she agreed sincerely; it was very sad.

'He should marry again,' she observed. 'It would be so much nicer for his little daughter too.'

'And for him,' observed her mother quietly. 'It must be difficult for him, especially with a child. But you won't be looking after her all the time, will you, dear? He said something about dealing with his English correspondence and giving a hand where it

was needed most. How very fortunate that you have
your St John Ambulance certificate.'

'I hardly think that I'll be expected to help out in
the surgery.' Prudence looked up from the letter she
was writing to Nancy. 'Heaven help the patients if I
do!'

She had forgotten to ask about the weather in
Holland, but surely Benedict would be biddable about
her coming back home to collect more clothes? She
packed skirts and blouses and a few woollies and a
couple of pretty dresses, and planned to travel in the
Jaeger suit she had just bought. Someone had told her
that it rained a lot in Holland and was almost always
windy, so she stowed her elderly Burberry in the boot
and added a handful of headscarves.

'Nothing for the evening, dear?' enquired her
mother.

Prudence looked doubtful. 'Well, I didn't think so—
I mean, I'm not a guest, you know.'

'But you're bound to meet some people.' Her
mother meant young men, of course. 'Why not take a
couple of those pretty chiffon blouses and your black
moiré skirt?'

The tickets arrived two days later—first class, she
noticed, and wondered if she was supposed to pay
Benedict back out of her salary. There was no note with
them, just a slip from a travel agency, but then he had
no reason to write.

She left home early in the morning to call first at
Highgate and say goodbye to Nancy and have an early
lunch with her before driving on to Harwich. It was
raining, a fine drizzle which dulled the countryside to
an overall mud colour, but Prudence didn't allow that
to worry her. True, she had hated saying goodbye to

her mother and father and Mabel, and Podge, uncannily aware that he would no longer get the long walks she took him each day, looked so forlorn that she felt like throwing the whole thing up and staying at home. But she didn't—after all, it wasn't for ever.

By the time she reached Nancy's flat the sun, rather on the watery side, had broken through the clouds, which somehow made all the difference, and Nancy made her feel even better.

'You know, Prudence, I'd envy you if I weren't married and perfectly happy. Just think, going to another country and working for someone as nice as Benedict! James says he's a splendid man.'

Prudence picked over the fruit in the centre bowl and chose a peach. 'Well, if he isn't I can always come back home!' she said flippantly.

She drove up to Harwich without haste; in any case the Mini just wasn't able to get up much of a speed, and once there she went unhurriedly about the business of getting herself and the Mini on board, and that done, had dinner and went to bed. She was a level-headed girl, despite the red hair. A good night's sleep was essential if she was to be at her best when she arrived in Appeldoorn. She woke early, had tea and toast in her cabin and had another look at the map. The trip didn't look too difficult and once she had reached that town all she had to do was to look out for the palace, Het Loo, take the left-hand turn at the crossroads and turn left again up a tree-lined avenue bordering the royal park. She dressed and went up on deck and found it raining again and Holland's coastline, flat and grey as the sky, only a few miles distant.

She had expected it to be flat, of course, but a few

more trees would have improved the skyline. She looked about her with interest as the ferry crept slowly into the quayside and then, obedient to the polite voice requesting drivers to rejoin their cars, went down to the car deck.

Customs and Passport control were slow but friendly and she found herself on the road, looking for the signpost to Rotterdam. Motorway for almost the whole trip, Benedict had told her, and rather dull, but by far the quickest way to travel.

He was probably right, decided Prudence, sandwiched between giant transports and very fast Mercedes, but there wasn't much pleasure in it, and it was a good thing that there wasn't much scenery, for she didn't dare take her eyes off the road for more than a few seconds at a time. What with driving on the wrong side of the road and getting used to dark blue signposts and traffic lights twice as high as those at home ... But presently, with Rotterdam safely negotiated, she relaxed. The motorway stretched before her and according to her map she would bypass almost every other town en route. The grey skies were getting lighter and presently a thin sunshine filtered through the clouds, turning the fields into a brilliant green and bringing to life the farms and villages. Prudence looked about her and decided that the country was charming in a peaceful, old-fashioned way. Once off the main roads, there might be a great deal to see. Beyond Gouda she remembered that she was hungry and pulled in at the next café, where she had coffee and a cheese roll. Probably there would be lunch when she arrived at Benedict's house.

Mindful of her instructions, she left the motorway just outside Arnhem and took the road north to

Appeldoorn, and the country was delightful. She slowed down so that she could take a good look at the woods and heath on either side of the road, and when she saw a picturesque restaurant standing back from the road, stopped for more coffee. This was where she would come on her free days, she determined; there were countless narrow sandy lanes leading away into the woods, just asking to be explored. She lingered longer than she had intended and was relieved to find that she was almost at the end of her journey.

She hadn't been particularly worried about finding Benedict's house; she wasn't the worrying kind and since the palace, Het Loo, was on the outskirts of the town, all she had to do was keep her eyes open. The palace stood well back from the road, linked to it by long tree-lined avenues and vast areas of grass, and once past this, she could see where she had to go; another avenue, also tree-lined, with the park on one side and on the other rather grand ornately built houses, each standing in large well kept grounds. The third one up from the road, Benedict had told her, and since its wrought iron gate was open she drove up the short sanded drive and stopped before the massive porch. Just for a moment she had a pang of sheer fright, squashed it firmly and got out, rang the ponderous bell beside the door and waited composedly.

A small round man answered the bell so quickly that she suspected that he might have been on the lookout for her. He was any age between fifty and seventy, quite bald and immensely dignified, but his smile was warm.

'Miss Trent, you will come in, please, and welcome. Dr van Vinke is in his study awaiting you.'

Thank God he speaks English, thought Prudence and followed him briskly down a long wide hall to a door at the end. Her companion, a few steps ahead of her, had almost reached it when it was opened and Benedict came out.

His hullo was friendly and casual—just as though, thought Prudence rather peevishly, I'd popped in from next door. 'No problems?' he asked, and didn't wait for her to answer. 'You'd like coffee while your bags are taken upstairs. Ork will see to them and put the car away.' He nodded to the round man, who murmured something and trotted off, while Benedict led the way back across the hall to double doors set in the panelled walls, opened them and invited her inside.

It was an impressive room, furnished with comfortable chairs and sofas. Some quite beautiful cabinets stood along its walls, a satinwood rent table between its two long windows and a very lovely Persian carpet on its polished wood floor. The velvet curtains were elaborately draped and echoed the muted colours of the carpet and the various chairs and sofas.

'Come and sit down,' invited Benedict. 'You had a good journey?'

'Splendid, thank you, though it needn't have rained quite so much.' She smiled at him; it was nice to see him again, he was a calm man and somehow soothing, and for some reason she was feeling ruffled. 'It's nice to be here, I only hope I'll be able to make myself useful.'

'No doubt of it. Here's the coffee and this is Sitska, my housekeeper and Ork's wife. Ork speaks English more or less, but she doesn't—that won't be a problem for long, you'll soon pick up a few useful words.

Sibella will be home presently—she goes to morning school and sometimes she goes to a friend's house to play until lunchtime.' And in answer to her questioning looks 'Next door—she is not allowed out on her own.'

He lounged back in his chair. 'Do pour the coffee.' And when she had: 'I've rounds to do this afternoon and then the hospital, if you like to unpack after lunch and get to know Sibella—take her for a walk, if you like. Ork will bring you tea when you want it, Sibella will bear you company until I get back, and if we can get an hour this evening, we'll discuss your—er—duties.'

He went on to ask about her family, putting her at her ease with his placid voice until the door opened and Sibella came in. She was small for her age, with her father's blue eyes and fair hair, cut short with a fringe. She had his calm too, crossing the room to kiss him and then slipping a hand in his while she studied Prudence. After a moment she said something to her father and smiled at them both.

Benedict laughed. 'She says you're very pretty.' He gave her a gentle push and spoke in Dutch and the child went to Prudence and offered a small paw.

'Hullo,' she said gravely.

'Hullo,' said Prudence, and smiled as she shook the hand and, wise after years of Sunday School classes, didn't say any more.

'I speak English,' volunteered Sibella.

'Oh, good. I can't speak Dutch, not one word.'

'I shall help you.' She went back to her father and climbed on to his knee. 'You will help also, Papa.'

'Oh, certainly I will.' He added something in Dutch and Sibella got off his knee. 'She'll take you to your room—you'll find Sitska already there, I believe.' He got to his feet. 'Lunch in ten minutes?'

She must remember that he was a busy man, Prudence told herself as she climbed the rather grand staircase behind the little girl and then accepted the hand held out to her as they reached the gallery which ran round three sides of the hall. They turned into a small passage through an archway and went into a room beyond, and Prudence uttered a cry of delight when she saw it. It was a fair size, with a bed of mahogany, matched with a bow-fronted table holding a triple mirror. There was a vast cupboard, two little easy chairs and pretty rose-coloured lamps on either side of a bowl of late roses. The carpet was thick and cream-coloured and the bedspread and curtains were flower-patterned chintz.

'Oh, this is delightful!' said Prudence, waltzing from the bed to the mirror-backed door leading to the bathroom and then to the window and the bedside table to examine the books thoughtfully laid upon it.

'You like?' asked Sibella.

'Oh, yes, my dear. It's beautiful.' Prudence got out a comb and her make-up and made short shrift of tidying herself, watched from the door by the little girl. She was turning away from the mirror when there was a tap on the half open door and the housekeeper bustled in. She was a tall, thin woman with a pleasant face who beamed at Prudence and then advanced to shake hands with her. 'Sitska,' she said, and added, 'Welcome'.

Prudence shook hands and smiled and murmured a quite useless 'How d'you do?' then waved a hand round the room. 'The room is charming,' she said, and tried again: 'Pretty . . .'

Sibella came to her rescue. 'Pretty—I know that word.' She entered into a lengthy conversation and Sitska smiled and nodded and then waved a hand towards the stairs. Presumably lunch was ready.

The dining room was on the opposite side of the hall to the drawing room. It held a large circular table capable of seating a dozen persons, as well as a great side table, chairs, and a William and Mary display cabinet whose glass-fronted shelves were filled with old Delft plates and dishes.

Benedict was standing at a window, a glass in his hand, but he turned round as they went in and offered Prudence a drink. 'Sorry to rush you, but my first appointment's in half an hour; you'll get used to my comings and goings—at least I hope you will.'

'It shouldn't be difficult,' said Prudence, 'Father's job isn't exactly nine to five!'

Lunch was a pleasant meal; cold meats and salad and a basket of breads of every kind, and accompanying these, hot creamy coffee. The talk was pleasant too, mostly about Appeldoorn and its history and the surrounding countryside. Benedict got up to go presently and Prudence, with Sibella in tow, went up to her room and unpacked.

This was a lengthy business, since Prudence had to explain her wardrobe garment by garment to Sibella, who, anxious to be helpful, told her the Dutch in return. By the time they had finished the rain had stopped and Benedict's suggestion of a walk seemed a good one, especially as they were joined on their way to the front door by a large woolly dog, intent on keeping them company. He was introduced as Henry, and a lead having been found, led them both at a brisk pace across the road and into the grass between the avenues leading towards the palace. Once there, he was released and set off on his own business, although he was obedient enough when he was called, something for which Prudence was thankful. Sibella was a chatterbox, quite undeterred by having to repeat almost everything she said two or three times; her boast that she could speak English wasn't quite true, although between them they carried on a lively conversation. Prudence was careful to keep talk to general things; although she was longing to ask questions about Benedict and his work and whether he went out a lot or entertained, but even if she had slipped in one or two leading questions she doubted if Sibella would have answered them. The child was friendly and anxious to please, but Prudence had the feeling that she would shut up like a clam if she wanted to.

They raced around the grass with Henry making a delighted third until they were all tired and Prudence suggested that they might go back for tea, a meal set ready for them in a small room behind the dining room, very cosy with a small fire burning in the old-fashioned grate and tea set out on a round table covered with a fringed tablecloth; rather Victorian but charming, Prudence decided, and sat down behind the teapot.

Someone had done their best to offer them an English tea; not the modern version of a cup of tea and a biscuit, but thin bread and butter, little cakes and scones. The pair of them ate with appetite while Henry sustained his hunger with crusts and bits of cake and a bowl of tea.

'You do not find it bad?' asked Sibella anxiously.

'Good gracious, no! I've got a dog called Podge, he always has his tea with us.'

'There are two cats, also—Miep and Poes. You like cats?'

'Very much,' said Prudence, and offered Henry a last morsel of cake and stood up. 'What would you like to do now?'

'You come to my . . .' Sibella's small face wrinkled in a heavy frown, '*speelkamer*,' and when Prudence only shook her head, took her hand and led her upstairs.

'Playroom,' said Prudence the moment she had put her head round the door. 'What fun! What shall we do?'

There was a doll's house on a table between the two windows, they pulled up chairs before it, opened its front door and became absorbed in its contents. It was a splendid thing with electric lights, and furnished down to the last spoon, and they went over it room by room; they were putting the inmates of the nursery on the second floor into their tiny beds when Benedict came quietly in.

He kissed his small daughter, patted Prudence's shoulder in an absentminded fashion and enquired as to their afternoon. Sibella, naturally enough, answered in Dutch. Prudence said carefully: 'I've enjoyed myself very much, I hope Sibella has too.' She stood up. 'I expect you like to be together for a while when you get home—if you tell me when you would like me to give Sibella her supper . . .?' It made her sound like a mid-Victorian governess, but she felt rather at sea.

Benedict chuckled. 'You're right, we usually spend an hour together about this time—I see private patients before dinner, but there's usually time to spare before then. Would you like to phone your mother? Use the telephone in my study, but do join us when you've done that; we might manage a wild game of Snakes and Ladders, it'll be more fun with three.'

Ork, appearing from nowhere, led the way to the study, opened the door for her, gave her a kindly smile and left her there. It was a large room with a partner's desk at one end of it, loaded with books and papers, and three of its walls were covered with book shelves; the third had a dark red paper and was covered, too, with paintings—family portraits, Prudence decided, going from one to the other. Stern-faced gentlemen with whiskers and high collars, mild-faced ladies in rich dresses, and over the hooded fireplace a large painting of an Edwardian lady. Benedict's mother? No, he wasn't as old as all that. His grandmother, perhaps. She was very pretty, and Prudence looked around to find her husband. He was high up on the wall, near the desk; it might have been Benedict with a flowing moustache and side whiskers. Their child would be there too, somewhere on the crowded wall, but she really hadn't the time to look. She sat down on the leather armchair behind the desk and made her call—a rather lengthy one, for her father had to be fetched from his study and her mother wasn't content with Prudence's rather sketchy description of the house and the people in it.

'I'll write,' promised Prudence. 'I'll post it tomorrow and you'll get it in a day or two—and I'll give you a ring once a week.'

And after that the evening passed pleasantly enough. While Benedict saw his patients, Prudence supervised Sibella's supper, then helped her bath and when she was ready for bed, went downstairs with her to the drawing room where Benedict was sitting, with Henry across his feet, reading the paper. He put it down as they went in and Sibella climbed on to his knee with the speed of time-honoured custom, so Prudence murmured gently and left them together. Dinner was at eight o'clock and there was still half an hour to go. She changed out of her suit and put on a thin wool dress, did her face and hair and got out her writing pad. She was halfway through her letter when she judged it time to go in search of Sibella and was rewarded by Benedict's look of approval.

'Did you know this infant goes to bed at ten minutes to eight, or was it a clever guess?'

'A guess—not very hard, because I did know that dinner is at eight o'clock,' she smiled. 'Is there anything special about going to bed? Does Sibella say goodnight here or do you go up . . .?'

'Oh, here, unless I've been held up and not got home early.' He kissed his small daughter and submitted to a throttling embrace. 'Come down as soon as you're ready,' he added. 'We can talk over dinner.'

The dinner table was elegant with lace mats, shining silver and sparkling glass. Ork served them with soup, roast pheasant and a chocolate mousse and poured claret for them to drink. Benedict lived in some style, but despite that, Prudence thought, the house had the casual well lived in comfort of home. It wasn't until they had gone back to the drawing room that he abandoned the gentle flow of small talk and said briskly: 'Now let's get down to business, shall we? I'll tell you what I would like you to do and you can find fault and make alterations when I've finished. We get up early—seven o'clock; surgery starts at eight o'clock, and I have to drive there. Sibella has breakfast with me at half past seven, and you will too, and then take her to school; it starts at half past eight. You will fetch her again at a quarter to twelve—she doesn't go in the afternoons. During the morning would you make yourself useful. Do the flowers, see to Sibella's clothes, open the post—I've got a secretary at my surgery, but a good deal of post comes here. Sort it out and let me have it when I get in. I'll skim through it and deal with the English letters if there are any. You'll have the afternoon with Sibella—with variations, of course; she goes to play with friends and they come here. You'll have precious little time to yourself, for while Sibella's at school you can fit in the letters. If you don't have time then, it'll have to be in the evening after dinner.' He paused and looked at her thoughtfully.

'Too much for you?' he asked.

'Certainly not. What else?'

'I've thought about your free time—how about Saturday afternoon and Sunday morning? We might have to change from time to time, though.'

'That will do nicely.' Prudence gave him a bright smile. She was going to earn every penny of her salary, as far as she could see she would be on the go from morning to night. But that was what she wanted, wasn't it? A job, something to do, something useful and demanding so that she could fill the hole Tony had left. She had done the right thing, she told herself silently, leaving the placid shelter of her home, where she might have stayed for the rest of her life if she hadn't made a push to change things. Perhaps she hadn't expected quite such a stern routine as Benedict had outlined in such a businesslike manner. It behoved her to be businesslike too and accept his challenge. She looked up and saw that he was watching her narrowly. Probably he expected her to wilt at the prospect he had set out before her; a young woman who had led a pleasant, easygoing life in a comfortable home. Her green eyes shone; she would show him—a challenge was just what she needed!

CHAPTER THREE

PRUDENCE had to admit to herself after the first few days, that in the challenge she had welcomed, she had bitten off just as much as she could chew. Sunday had presented no problems; Benedict had told her that she was free to do as she chose until lunchtime, but if she would like to accompany him and Sibella to church she was welcome. So she had gone to church with them, to sit in a high pew between them, with Sibella shrilling away at the hymns and Benedict, several octaves lower, deafening her on the other side. But she had enjoyed it; the service was not unlike the one she was used to, even though she didn't understand a word of it, and her father would be interested to read about it. She sat through the very long sermon, wondering what the afternoon held in store for her.

A drive round Appeldoorn and its surroundings so that she would be able to find her way, sitting beside Benedict with Sibella squeezed between them. The town was delightful with its broad tree-lined streets, colourful now with the leaves already tinted with red and yellow, and the surrounding villages; Loenen with its sixteenth-century castle, the echoing well at Soeren, Beekbergen with its old church and Ugchelen with its springs and wide moorland. They stopped for tea in Loenen and took a roundabout way home so that Prudence could see as much as possible as they went. And in the evening there had been friends in for drinks. Sibella, because it was Sunday, was allowed to stay up for an hour longer and sat still as a mouse beside Prudence, watching her father's guests. Prudence, quietly elegant in one of the wool dresses, made no attempt to draw attention to herself, although her red hair and extraordinary eyes caused a good deal of interest. Benedict was meticulous in introducing her to everyone, but she was so quiet and retiring in her manner that his guests decided that while she was a very pretty girl and pleasant, she wasn't very exciting—exactly the impression she had wished to convey. She had stationed herself beside Sibella, quietly watching the company. The women were for the most part young, smart and married to the rather sober men there. Only a handful stood out from the rest; young and not quite so young, dressed in the latest fashions regardless of expense, their hair tinted and styled to perfection, their make-up delicately perfect.

Prudence admired them without envy and answered readily enough when one or other of them stopped to talk to her for a few minutes. Any one of them, she decided would make an excellent wife for Benedict, but he showed no particular preference for any of them—but then, she suspected, she knew he wasn't a man to show his feelings in public.

And afterwards, when she had put Sibella to bed, listening to the sound of cars being driven away from the house, she went downstairs again and found that she was to dine alone. The doctor, Ork told her, had accepted a last-minute invitation to dine with some friends and begged she would excuse him.

So she ate her meal at the large table, feeling lost in the formal room, reminding herself that Benedict was perfectly at liberty to do exactly what he wished; indeed, hadn't he employed her so that he might have more time for himself? She went to bed rather early, after wishing Ork a composed goodnight.

It wasn't difficult to get up early the next morning; she had always done so at home—besides, she had slept soundly all night. She went along to Sibella's room when she was ready, and together they went downstairs to find Benedict already at table, opening a pile of letters and drinking coffee. He wished them both good morning, begged his daughter not to strangle him as she hugged him and told Prudence to help herself to whatever she wanted.

There was plenty to choose from; rolls and toast and croissants, cheese, jam and marmalade and boiled eggs. She served Sibella and herself and looked at his empty plate.

'And you, Dr van Vinke?' she asked.

He looked up briefly from his letters. 'Oh, anything—I've not much time.'

So she buttered toast and put it on his plate, cut the top off an egg and poured him another cup of coffee. He ate and drank in an absentminded fashion and when he had finished his letters observed: 'There are several letters for you, Prudence; there'll be time to see to them directly after lunch. There's a small room next to my study with a desk and a typewriter—you can work there.' He got up, dropped a kiss on Sibella's head and laid the letters beside Prudence's plate. 'Get them sorted, will you?'

So her morning had been fully occupied, what with getting Sibella to school, ten minutes' walk away, and then being met in the hall by Sitska, who insisted that she should go round the house with Ork trailing behind acting as interpreter. 'So that you will not feel lost,' he pointed out kindly.

The house was large with a surprisingly large number of rooms. Prudence, if she hadn't been worrying about the letters, would have enjoyed herself enormously. Besides the rooms she had already seen, there was a small sitting room behind the drawing room, a vast conservatory running the width of the house at the back, a large kitchen with a pantry and utility room and a back stairs, and on the floor above, a number of large beautifully furnished bedrooms with dressing rooms and bathrooms. And still higher, several smaller rooms reached by a circular staircase, and at the back of the house, the flat where Ork and Sitska lived. It was well after eleven o'clock by the time they had finished peering into all the rooms, and Prudence, coffee cup in hand, hurried to the room she had been told of and sat down behind the desk to sort out the letters. There were several bills, two requests for Benedict to lecture in Bristol and Edinburgh, a bank statement which she left in its envelope and an invitation from someone called Thelma, asking him to stay next time he was in England. She was a bit uneasy about reading this one, but after all, he had given them to her to sort out, and thank heaven that he had; at least she had some idea of the replies she would have to take down later on.

She arranged them neatly, put paper ready, found a notebook and pencil and tried out the typewriter. Pray heaven he wouldn't use any long words!

What time there was left before lunch was completely taken up with fetching Sibella, smartening her up for lunch and then going downstairs to meet Benedict coming into the house.

He kissed his small daughter, asked Prudence to

pour him a drink and get one for herself and supposed
that she had had a quiet morning.

'Very pleasant, thank you,' said Prudence quietly,
and he went on:

'I've someone I must see before I go to the hospital
after lunch—I'd like to get those letters dealt with
before I leave.'

Lunch was a cheerful meal, but no time was wasted,
Sibella was sent to the kitchen with Sitska and
Prudence repaired to her little room, fetched the
letters and her notebook and presented herself in
Benedict's study.

He was businesslike to the point of brusqueness, but
thank heaven he had no taste for long letters.
Somehow she had managed to take down his replies,
promised, rashly, to have them ready for him when he
got back late that afternoon, and made a note of the
phone calls that he wished to make when he got home.
And once he had gone, she went along to find Sibella.
It was a fine afternoon, even if chilly, and a walk with
Henry was priority number one.

By dint of cutting her teatime to a minimum and
leaving Sibella in Sitska's charge for a time, Prudence
was able to get the letters finished, but only just.
When Benedict got home, she was on her way to the
kitchen to fetch Sibella, looking a little flushed and
with her red hair ruffled round her pretty face.

'You look as though you've been busy,' observed
Benedict. He looked faintly disbelieving as he spoke,
so that she was forced to deny that she had had
anything much to do, telling herself silently that it
would be much easier once her typing and shorthand
had improved.

Her work had been all right, though, and she had

gone to bed after another solitary dinner feeling that she had achieved something.

The next two days were of the same pattern, except that Benedict had been home for dinner, a leisurely meal that she had enjoyed. They had a lot in common, she had discovered, and once or twice she had quite forgotten that she was working for him in a humble capacity, and, remembering, had suffered acute unease after some particularly forthright statement in disagreement with him. But she had decided not to stay downstairs after dinner, and indeed, the decision was unnecessary, because he didn't ask her to. His goodnights were friendly but definite and she presumed that he spent his evenings in his study or reading.

It was on the third day that things were a little different. There had been more letters than previously, so Prudence was hard put to it to get them done by the time he got home, and indeed, there were still two to type and no chance to do them before dinner, for Sibella had demanded that the three of them should play cards until it was her supper time, so that when Prudence came downstairs after putting her to bed and tidying herself for the evening, she was met in the hall by Benedict with a mild: 'You haven't finished the letters?'

'Two more—I'm sorry I haven't got them done. I'll type them now while you're having your drink.'

He smiled at her very nicely. 'Indeed you will not. Time enough after dinner, surely? I shan't be going out this evening, you can let me have them before you go to bed.' He glanced at her. 'I'm not working you too hard? Sibella must take up a good deal of your time.'

He was far too kind to ask her what she did with her
mornings while the child was at school, and it would
sound as though she was making excuses if she told him
that she had taken over several little jobs from Sitska
round the house; jobs that the daily woman wasn't
allowed to do; the silver and glass had to be cleaned and
polished, and although Ork usually did that, if he was
busy in the garden it left him little leisure if he had the
whole lot to do. But of course, Benedict wouldn't know
that and no one was going to tell him. Prudence had no
doubt that if and when he married again, his wife would
see to it that there was more help in the house. The
flowers alone took hours to do.

All the same, she was enjoying life. It was what she
had wanted, to be busy, feel that she was needed,
doing something useful. She had agreed quietly to
finish the letters after dinner and gone to sit with
Benedict for the pleasant few minutes before dinner—
a few minutes she did find herself looking forward to.

She was at her desk presently, putting the first sheet
into the typewriter, when she heard the clang of the
doorbell and Ork cross the hall to answer the door.
The caller was a woman. Prudence, typing briskly,
tried not to listen to the tinkling laughter and the
rather high-pitched voice followed by Benedict's deep
tones. The voices faded and a door closed; they had
gone into the drawing room. She finished her letters
and then sat for a minute or two wondering what to
do. Leave them on the desk? Take them along to
Benedict's study? She had her hand on the study door
when he came out of the drawing room.

'Finished? Good—I was just coming to find you.
Come and meet Myra again—she was here the other
evening, but I suspect that you won't remember her.'

Prudence remembered her very well—a tall, curvy girl with ash-blonde hair, rather startling eye make-up and clothes bought regardless of expense. They shook hands warily and Myra laughed her tinkling laugh and said: 'Oh, I remember you very well—your hair, you understand, it is so very red.'

To which Prudence said nothing, only allowed her green eyes to linger on the other girl's artfully tinted locks with an eloquence which spoke volumes. Benedict hid his smile. 'Won't you have a drink?' he invited, his voice very placid.

'No, thanks—I want to get a letter finished before I go to bed, so I'll say goodnight, if you won't think me rude.' She smiled at Myra. 'Nice seeing you again— and what is it you say? *Tot ziens.*' She glanced at Benedict. 'Goodnight, Doctor.'

She went to the door and he went ahead of her to open it. She didn't look at him as she went past, which was a pity; the look on his face would have given her food for thought—amusement, gentle mockery? A little of both.

She made no attempt to write letters when she reached her room, but went and sat down in one of the armchairs pulled up to the window. The house was too solidly built for her to hear voices downstairs, but that didn't stop her wondering what Benedict and his pretty visitor were talking about. 'Brazen creature!' muttered Prudence waspishly, and got up to run a bath, telling herself that it was no concern of hers who Benedict had for a friend—indeed, she had absolutely no interest in him whatever. That he was kind and placidly goodnatured, she had to admit, although he was proving a much harder taskmaster than she had supposed he would be, but beyond that she couldn't care less. He had been the means of getting her away from a too sheltered life at home, and from Tony; she was grateful for that.

Benedict wasn't at breakfast the next morning; Ork told them in his strangely accented, sparse English that he had been called out in the early hours of the morning. 'He leaves letter for me,' he explained. He shrugged. 'I do not know when he comes.'

He came ten minutes later in slacks and a sweater, with a bristly chin and lines of tiredness etched into his face. He came in quietly, wished them good morning in his usual placid manner, begged to be allowed to eat his breakfast before making himself presentable, and sat down.

Curiosity got the better of Prudence. 'Did you have to go to the hospital or just a patient?'

Benedict wolfed down the best part of a croissant. 'A patient—he's in hospital now.'

'He'll get better?'

'I'll give him a fifty-fifty chance.' He passed his cup for more coffee and said mildly: 'I didn't know you were interested in medical matters, Prudence?'

Something behind the mildness made her glance at him. She said quickly: 'I don't mean to be nosey, and I am interested.' She looked away from the blue eyes staring at her. 'It was thoughtless of me; you're tired, the last thing you would want to talk about is your work . . .'

'On the contrary, Prudence, you would be surprised to know that there are times when I come home and long for someone to talk to; an ear to fill with my doubts and petty annoyances and small triumphs.'

Sibella had been listening, more than half understanding. Then she piped something urgent to her

father. He smiled kindly and shook his head,
answering her gently.

'Sibella asks why I cannot confide in her—I have
told her that she isn't quite old enough . . .' He paused
as the child interrupted him. 'She suggests, most
sensibly, that I should marry someone—just so long as
she approves of her.' He opened the first of his letters
and glanced up from it. 'What do you think about
that, Prudence?'

She said sedately: 'I imagine it might be an excellent
idea, but I can hardly judge, can I?' And when he
pushed the pile of letters towards her she began to
open them neatly with the paper knife Ork never failed
to put on the breakfast table, but when she passed the
open envelopes back to him Benedict pushed them on
one side. 'I'm late already,' he said. 'Get them sorted,
will you—keep the English ones for later and leave the
others on the table in the hall, I'll pick them up as I
go.'

He got up, kissed Sibella and with a friendly nod to
Prudence, went away. Sibella hadn't quite finished her
breakfast, so she had time, but only just, to pile the
letters neatly before walking to school with her.
Benedict hadn't appeared before they left. Prudence
supposed she wouldn't see him again all day; he had
said something about not being home for lunch, a
remark which for some reason she had found
depressing. She gave herself a mental shake and
embarked on one of the long rambling conversations
which Sibella so enjoyed. Walking back presently, she
planned her day. There was plenty to keep her
occupied; Sitska had promised to take her shopping,
there was Henry to take for a run, the letters to attend
to, a dress of Sibella's which needed shortening. It was

surprising how much she enjoyed the mundane jobs that filled her days. Not for the world would she admit to herself that she was, just now and then, lonely.

The shopping was fun. Since Sitska spoke no English and Prudence, beyond half a dozen words, spoke no Dutch, it took rather longer than it should have done; the dress would have to wait until the evening, she decided as she raced across the grass with Henry, throwing sticks for his benefit. He came and sat with her in her little room while she sat at the desk reading the letters. If she knew what they were about it made it much easier when she came to take down the replies, and Benedict seemed to take it for granted that she should see them all. They were almost always bills relating to the flat he apparently used when he was in London, dry-as-dust letters from other medical men, appeals from charities and requests for him to attend some meeting or other. A busy man. She wondered, for all his calm manner, if he was a happy one. True, he had a delightful home, enough money and Sibella and quite possibly several more girl-friends like Myra. 'Horrid creature!' declared Prudence loudly, and startled Henry from his snoozing.

They were having tea round the small fire Ork had lit in the playroom when Benedict walked in, followed by Sitska with more tea.

'Buttered toast!' he exclaimed. 'And sandwiches and cake! Just what I could do with.' He took the cup of tea Prudence had poured for him. 'What a heavenly time Henry's having—he'll get fat.'

'Well, he's taken us for a long, long walk this afternoon, he really deserves a bit of toast. You've had a busy day?'

'Yes. How's school, Sibella?' His voice was friendly enough, but she could recognise a snub when she got one. She really must remember that she was a paid member of his household and act accordingly. She sat listening to Sibella's chatter, not understanding it, concentrating on plans for her half day on Saturday. She would take the car and drive somewhere, do some shopping and have tea out and perhaps a cinema in the evening. If she had a half day, was she allowed to have dinner as usual or was she supposed to stay out? And who on earth was she going to ask about that? She had been so pleased at the idea of having half of Saturday and Sunday morning to herself, but there were a number of things . . . what about breakfast and lunch on Sunday? . . .

'You're looking worried, Prudence.' Benedict's voice cut across her thoughts and she said instantly:

'Well, I'm not, thank you. Do you want to do the letters before dinner or later on—there aren't many.'

'Oh, before dinner, I think. Perhaps Sibella could have her supper with Sitska while we brush through them.' He gave her a thoughtful look. 'I expect you'd like half an hour to yourself while Sibella and I play Racing Demon.'

'Of course. I'll take the tray with me.' She escaped thankfully.

By the time she had got everything ready for Sibella's bedtime, pinned up the dress for sewing later, and added a few lines to the letter she was writing home, it was time to fetch the little girl for her supper, and then go along to the office, collect her notebook and pencil and tap on the study door.

Benedict was already there writing at his desk. He looked up briefly and asked: 'What have we got?' and held out a hand. Prudence sat down on a chair near the desk, notebook open and pencil poised, looking, she hoped, the picture of efficiency, and indeed, for the first three letters she was in fine form, but the fourth letter was from a doctor and Benedict's reply was full of long medical terms beyond her primitive shorthand. She had to stop him twice and ask him how to spell diverticulitis and, worse, fibroelastosis. He answered her patiently, but she saw the small frown on his face which made her panicky, so that when she had to ask yet again if rachitis had two t's or one, he paused in his dictating to observe:

'I can quite see that the medical terms are difficult for you, Prudence, but surely the simpler words aren't beyond you?'

She put down her pencil with a hand which shook. Try as she might, her voice shook a little too. She said tartly: 'Dr van Vinke, I'm employed by you as a kind of general assistant, not as a highly proficient shorthand-typist. I'm doing my best!' She almost added, And if you don't like it you can sack me, but bit the words back in time. But other words came tumbling out, things she had been thinking and wanted to say. 'You're a busy man, and a clever one, I have no doubt, with no time to spare on mundane things, but you've—you've flung me in at the deep end. Oh, I know you've told me what my duties are, but I daresay you've no idea how anyone sets about them and the time it takes. I'm not whining that I have too much to do, but it's all strange to me—the life, the language, working for someone . . . I've never done that before, you see, and I expect that's why I'm slow and awkward.'

He had sat back in his chair, quietly watching her.

Now he asked: 'You regret coming? You aren't happy with us?'

'Oh, but I am—you've no idea ... Sibella is a darling and Sitska and Ork are so kind, even the daily help ... and it's lovely to be busy all day, not just doing the flowers or going to the village shop or typing Father's sermons and knowing that there was only Tony ...' She stopped and Benedict said quietly: 'Go on.'

'I think I mean that nothing was exciting any more.' She thought for a moment. 'There was nothing to get my teeth into.'

Benedict got up and came round the desk and sat on its edge in front of her. 'I'm glad we've cleared the air, and you're quite right, I flung you into the deep end with hardly a backward glance. You see, I knew you'd cope; you are coping so well that I quite forgot that you aren't a first class secretary, that you don't understand a word of our language, that you have to find everything out for yourself with the aid of a dictionary. I daresay any other girl would have fled screaming by now.' He turned to look out of the window. 'I'm sorry, Prudence, will you forgive me?'

'Well, I don't see that I have anything to forgive. It must be quite ghastly to have to stop and spell words and answer silly questions when you've so much on your mind.'

Benedict grinned at her. 'For a girl with red hair and green eyes you've got a lot of common sense.'

'What's so strange about that?' asked Prudence.

'Well, you don't need it really, do you? You can get by on your looks.' He added deliberately: 'Tony must have been mad to let you go.'

'I let him go, if you remember.'

'And you don't regret that either?'

She gave him a level look. 'No. Would you like these before dinner?'

'Please. Before you go, Prudence, there's something you should know; I believe we're in for a whooping cough epidemic; there are already more than the usual number of cases for this time of the year and so many parents have neglected to have their children immunised.' He paused, and Prudence asked quickly:

'Sibella?'

'She'll be all right, she's had her jabs, but keep an eye on her. She can still get it, but only slightly.' He looked suddenly tired. 'It's the other children I'm so worried about.'

'Are you a paediatrician? I thought you had a practice . . .?'

'Oh, I have, but I'm not a children's doctor. But there are any number of children coming to the clinic.'

Prudence said, 'Oh, I see,' although she didn't really, and then: 'I'll go along and see if Sibella's finished her supper. Is there anything else you'd like me to do before dinner?'

'No, thanks. I'll have to go out again presently, but we'll have dinner first.'

When Sibella was safely tucked up in bed, Prudence went along to her own room. She changed, as she had done each evening so far, into one of the wool dresses and then, with rather more care than usual, did her face and brushed her fiery head until it gleamed. She didn't look too bad, she told her reflection in the looking glass—not that Benedict would notice; he looked at her, of course, but with a casual friendliness which did nothing for her ego. But that was just what made working for him so nice, she mused, going downstairs.

Over dinner they talked; they shared a lot of common interests and those they didn't they argued about, Benedict with placid good sense tinged with amusement, Prudence in her usual hotheaded fashion, and it made for a very enjoyable meal. They were sitting over their coffee when Benedict asked: 'What do you plan to do on Saturday afternoon?'

'I thought I'd take the car and drive around a bit—I came through some very pretty country, I'd like to explore it.'

'A good idea. Why not take the whole day? And in the evening?'

She hesitated. Should she ask about having dinner as usual or should she say that she was going to stay out for the evening? The prospect of finding somewhere to eat and having a meal on her own wasn't inviting.

Benedict was watching her face. He said smoothly: 'If you're not doing anything much, I'm having a few old friends for dinner, I'd like you to come as my guest.' He sat back in his chair. 'Sitska will get Sibella to bed and see to her supper and so on.'

Prudence stared back at him thoughtfully. 'Are you just being kind?' she wanted to know.

'Certainly not, and I think you'll like the people who are coming.'

'Well then—yes, I'd love to!' She added with engaging candour: 'I was wondering what to do about meals . . .'

'I should have thought of that. Come and go as you please when you are free, though once you've got to know a few people I daresay you'll get asked out from time to time.' He studied her expressive face and went on: 'Sibella and I were wondering if you would like to come with us on Sunday—I know the morning is your own, but we rather thought we'd go out to lunch. There is a nice place on the road to Amersfoort?'

'Thank you, but won't I be . . . well, you don't get Sibella to yourself very much, do you?'

'As much as any other father, I imagine. Will you come?'

She agreed. Suddenly the weekend promised to be rather fun.

The weather was turning colder, but the sky was blue and the sun shone when she got up on Saturday morning. She was out of the house soon after nine o'clock without seeing either Sibella or Benedict, who, Ork told her, had gone riding together. And that was another possibility, Prudence thought, getting into her car and driving carefully out of the town.

There were odds and ends of shopping she intended doing, and since Benedict had said that they would be going towards Amersfoort on Sunday, she chose to go in the other direction, to Zutphen. It was no distance, twelve miles or so along a main road which still contrived to be delightful, and once parked in the town, she wandered around its twisting streets, admiring the gabled houses and gateways. And presently, after coffee in an elegant café, she went along to Saint Wallburg Church to inspect its chained library and afterwards went to a hotel close by Gravenhof for lunch—a wildly expensive meal, but after all, she had spent very little money so far. She did her shopping next, taking her time and then having tea before driving back to Appeldoorn. She had enjoyed her afternoon and it was nice to have something to do with her evening.

She garaged the car in the converted stables at the back of the house, sliding it carefully between Benedict's super model and a small, not very new Renault. There were bicycles in one corner too and a long wooden shelf against the furthest wall holding an assortment of tennis racquets, skates, skis, carefully covered, and an inflatable dinghy. Except for the skis, they were all in need of small repairs and a good clean. Prudence, peering at them, decided that one day, when she had the time, she would give them all a good going over; they were all of them expensive and it was a sinful waste to leave them lying there.

It so happened that when she went into the house through the garden door she bumped into Benedict, on his way out. With the merest hint of a hullo she plunged into the matter. 'Those skates and things in the garage—they're far too good to leave lying around—they need a clean . . .' She stopped, because he was laughing at her. 'What's so funny about that?' she wanted to know tartly.

'You sound like a wife—you see what happens when a man lives on his own!'

'But you don't—there's Ork and Sitska and Betje and old Mevrouw Smit and the garden boy . . .'

'And you, Prudence. You're filling a gap very nicely.' He smiled down at her. 'Dinner's at eight o'clock, but come down for drinks first, won't you? Have you had a good day?'

'Lovely. You went riding?'

'Yes, Sibella has her own little pony—we stable him and my own horse just outside the town. Do you ride, Prudence?'

She went red. 'Well, yes.' She glanced at him

through long lashes. 'I wasn't fishing, truly I wasn't, and if you suggest that I should go riding, I'll refuse.'

'So we'll say no more about it,' he said gently, to her great discomfort. 'See you later.'

There was an envelope on the dressing table in her room with a typed statement and one week's wages. It looked a great deal in Dutch guldens and for a moment it diverted her thoughts from Benedict, but not for long. A good man to work for; kind and thoughtful, but remarkably casual at times, and always expecting one to work just that little bit harder. He worked too hard himself, of course. He ought to marry again, she decided as she lay in a too hot bath, but not that awful girl Myra—someone calm and sensible who would love Sibella and see that he didn't overtax his strength. No, that was silly. Benedict had the kind of strength that never got overtaxed. Prudence began to dress, thankful that her mother had persuaded her to put in the evening skirt and several blouses. She chose a cream chiffon one with a high pie-frill neck and deep cuffed sleeves. It had a tucked front and tiny pearl buttons and was a splendid background for her hair and eyes.

She went downstairs just after half past seven, to find Benedict in his chair reading a newspaper, a glass on the table beside him. He got up and pulled a smaller chair closer to the cheerful fire. 'Have a drink,' he suggested, 'and I'll tell you about the people who are coming. They all speak English, by the way, so you won't have to sit around looking like a beautiful stranded goldfish.' He ignored her look and went on blandly: 'Two colleagues of mine and their wives, my godmother, an old lady in full possession of her wits, and a professor of surgery from the hospital. They're all nice people, at least I think so, and we share the same opinion on a number of things, don't we?'

'Do we? I hadn't thought.'

'No? But we agreed wholeheartedly about men who weren't jealous when their girl-friends spent too much time talking to other men.'

'There is no need . . .' began Prudence, her voice rather high, and was interrupted by Ork at the door announcing Dr and Mevrouw Brand.

They were Benedict's age, the Doctor a little thin on top already, his long thin face lighted by a warm smile, his wife made up for his thin length by being large and cosily plump, with a round face and bright dark eyes. Within two minutes Prudence felt quite at home with them, and it was the same with the next guests to arrive, Dr and Mevrouw Penninck, a good deal younger and both good-looking. They were all talking with the ease of old friends when Mevrouw van der Culp was announced.

She was small and thin, with white hair beautifully dressed and bright blue eyes, wearing something black and elegant, her fingers sparkling with rings. She kissed Benedict as though she really enjoyed it, greeted the others and looked at Prudence. 'Introduce this beautiful creature,' she commanded, and Benedict did so. 'I hope you'll be very happy, my dear,' she observed, 'working for Benedict. He's a slavedriver, you know, but you look quite capable of dealing with him.'

Prudence murmured politely, not at all sure what to say. The old lady was rather a dear and she thought she was going to like her, but it would hardly do for her to comment about Benedict. She was saved from enlarging on her mumbling by the arrival of the last

guest. Professor Herrisma was of middle height and
thickset, with a handsome face and greying hair. He
knew everyone there and while he was greeting
Prudence she had a chance to look at him. She liked
what she saw, and she liked him even better when
Benedict introduced him to her and he stayed to talk
for a few minutes. They didn't say much, the usual
questions and answers about her arrival and whether
she liked Appeldoorn and where did she live in
England, but she was left with the feeling that she
would like to know him better.

The dinner table being round, conversation was for
the most part general. Prudence, between Dr Brand
and Professor Herrisma, enjoyed every word of it. She
enjoyed the food too, and the glass of Burgundy she
had with the roast pheasant served to put her into
excellent spirits. All the same, she made no effort to
attract attention: that would never do.

They sat around and talked later, and no one went
home until past midnight, and then reluctantly. And
by then they were all calling her Prudence and she had
invitations to go to lunch on the following two
weekends, and as Mevrouw van der Culp left she
signified her intention of taking Prudence to Arnhem
before the weather worsened. 'There's a great deal to
see there, child,' she said in her clear voice, 'and some
splendid shops. I live just outside the city, so it will be
easy enough to come and fetch you.'

'I have a car,' said Prudence. 'I expect I could drive
to your home if you would like that.'

'Excellent. Something shall be arranged.' She
turned to Benedict. 'Give my love to Sibella, my
dear—you must all come over for tea one Sunday.'

Professor Herrisma went last of all because there

was some small matter he and Benedict wanted to discuss, but when Prudence wished them both goodnight, Benedict said: 'Don't go, we shall only be a few minutes.' So she went back to the drawing room and sat by the dying fire, nicely drowsy.

They were as good as their word; they were back within ten minutes, although they didn't sit down. After a few minutes' desultory talk Professor Herrisma bade them goodnight. 'A delightful evening, Benedict, and many thanks.' He took Prudence's hand and shook it carefully as though it might break. 'I hope we shall meet again, Prudence. If you are interested in hospitals I shall be delighted to show you round the surgical side—perhaps you could manage an afternoon next week?' He smiled into her eyes. 'And do please call me Everard—to be called Professor makes me feel fatherly, and I assure you that I do not feel in the least paternal!'

Prudence, aware that Benedict was listening, smiled delightfully. 'I should love to go over the hospital, though the afternoons are a bit awkward.'

She was interrupted by Benedict's cheerful: 'Oh, I'm sure we can spare you for a couple of hours. Doesn't Sibella have dancing class on Wednesdays? That should give you a couple of hours.'

'Well then, thank you Pro . . . Everard.'

She was crossing the hall to go upstairs when Benedict came from the porch, shutting the great door behind him. 'Well, well,' he remarked with a wicked gleam in his eyes, 'my old friend seems to have taken a fancy to you, Prudence. He's been a bachelor for the best part of forty years, but you seem to have caught his eye.'

She had stopped by the stairs. For some reason she

was put out—more than that, furious. 'Don't be vulgar,' she begged him. 'I think Everard is a very nice person and I'm glad I met him. And I'm delighted that he's asked me to go round the hospital with him.'

Benedict crossed the hall and came to stand in front of her. 'What a touchy girl you are,' he observed mildly. 'I suppose it's the red hair.' He bent suddenly and kissed her cheek. 'I think somehow your future is settled for you, Prudence. Now go to bed.'

She couldn't think of an answer to that, so she went, not looking back.

CHAPTER FOUR

PRUDENCE didn't sleep very well, she was in fact nicely tired, but the annoying thought that Benedict hadn't suggested that she might like to see round the hospital kept her awake. He had welcomed Everard's invitation with the greatest good humour, but somehow it rankled that he hadn't been the first to suggest it. There was no reason why he should suggest it, of course. There was another reason why she couldn't get to sleep—what on earth had Benedict meant about her future being settled? He surely wasn't thinking that Everard Herrisma was seriously interested in her. Love at first sight was something best left to novels; she and Tony had been friends for some time before he had even hinted at marrying her, and although she had been more than half in love with him, she couldn't recall being swept off her feet. The whole idea was absurd, and if Benedict hadn't made such a silly remark she wouldn't have given it another thought; just because you were attracted to someone and he to you it didn't mean that you were going to plunge into marriage or even an affair.

She slept at last, disturbed by dreams which tantalisingly faded the moment she woke up.

As it was Sunday, breakfast was a rather more leisurely meal and since church wasn't until ten o'clock, Prudence had time to herself afterwards while Benedict and Sibella took Henry for his walk. She wandered upstairs to her room, finished a letter, poked at her hair and did her nails again, wishing that she was with the others, but she hadn't been invited, presumably because Benedict supposed she wanted to be on her own since it was her free morning. Standing at the window, watching the trees behind the house bending and bowing to the wind, she wondered if she could do something about it; it was strange, but she felt a little aimless. She liked the busy days and even though she had enjoyed her outing to Zutphen she had felt rather lonely; it would have been fun to have had a companion to talk to. Perhaps Benedict would agree to her dropping her free half days and just taking an hour or two off for shopping when they could be fitted in.

A subdued bustle in the hall indicated that they were back, and a moment later Henry came racing upstairs and pushed into her bedroom door. Following him came Sibella.

The child flung herself at Prudence. 'I like it when you are with me.' She picked up Prudence's jacket from the bed. 'Now we go to church.'

They drove there in the Aston Martin, and after the service and an interval of brief chat amongst people Benedict knew in the congregation, they drove out of the town, down a broad, tree-lined road with glimpses of country houses on either side, their grounds merging into the woods beyond.

Prudence, stretching her pretty neck to see everything, remarked on the charm of their surroundings. 'It must be lovely to live here, but I like your house too, although it's too large for you ...' She stopped and went pink. 'So sorry, I didn't mean to be rude.'

Benedict glanced at her sideways. He said quietly: 'Another good reason why I should take a wife, and then before she could reply: 'That hideous brick house on your left, a perfect example of mid-Victorian taste, belongs to Everard—now there's a man who needs a wife too.'

Something in his voice made her peep quickly at him. His profile was calm and unsmiling. All the same, she blushed again.

The restaurant wasn't far. De Echoput was well known for its excellent food and most of the tables were already occupied, but Benedict had booked and they were led to one at once in a corner window with a splendid view of the restaurant itself as well as the charming grounds surrounding it. That Benedict was known there was obvious, for Sibella was made much of, allowed to choose what she wanted whether it was on the menu or not, and given a glass of lemonade while her elders made their choice over their own drinks. Even in Dutch money, everything was wildly expensive, and Prudence searched fruitlessly for something reasonable. Benedict, watching her over his own menu, smiled very faintly. 'I'm going to have lobster soup—and I suggest that you have the same, Prudence, and they do a delicious duckling in brandy sauce. I don't know about you, but all that singing has made me hungry!'

Thankfully she agreed and turned her attention to Sibella, who couldn't make up her mind between chicken in a cream sauce or steak tartare.

'I should have the chicken, we had steak for dinner only a day or so ago. Look, they've got aubergines, you like those.'

It was a pleasant meal, any gaps in the conversation being instantly filled with Sibella's chatter, and presently, since the afternoon was still fine, they drove on, turning off into a side road after a mile or two towards Barneveld and then taking a country road across the Veluwe towards Dieren.

Benedict drove slowly through the narrow lanes, sometimes hemmed in on all sides by dense woods, sometimes with nothing but heath all round them.

'It's a bit like the New Forest,' said Prudence.

'Yes—nice, isn't it? And right on our doorstep. It's quite something in the winter when we've had snow.' Then he turned to smile at her. 'Shall we have tea out or go home and have a picnic round the fire?'

'Oh, home,' said Prudence. Benedict's faint smile came and went. 'Right. We'll turn off here and wander back through the woods towards Hoenderloo and pick up the road there.'

'It must be easy to get lost here,' observed Prudence.

'If you leave the main roads, yes. Having lived here all my life I know it well—there are any number of lanes like this one if only you know where to find them. Most people keep to the roads, and you can't blame them.' He slowed down at a tiny village. 'If you drive down here, Prudence, ask me for a map.'

They had their tea round the fire in the drawing room, with a lamp or two and the flickering flames turning the room into a lovely homely haven. It was a pity that the peace of it had to be broken by Benedict's brisk: 'I'll be out this evening, but not until Sibella's in bed. You'll be able to amuse yourself, Prudence?'

'Yes, thanks. I've got heaps to do.'

'Good. Ork and Sitska will be out, but Betje will be here if you want anything.'

She went to bed early. The house, despite vague kitchen sounds from Betje on the other side of the

baize door, seemed too quiet. She read for a bit and
presently dropped off to sleep, to be wakened by
someone laughing. Myra. Prudence sat up in bed, her
ears unashamedly stretched to their limit, but all she
could hear was a car starting up and driving away and
a moment later the sound of a door being gently
closed. She lay down again, punched her pillows into
greater comfort and reminding herself that it was none
of her business, anyway, closed her eyes firmly and
went back to sleep.

The second week was much like the first, only now
she had found her feet and things came more easily,
and on Wednesday, true to his word, Everard
Herrisma telephoned and arranged to meet her at the
hospital in the afternoon. The previous week Ork had
driven them to the dancing lesson, but now Prudence
decided to take Sibella in her own car, and after seeing
the child safely there, got in again and drove herself
to the hospital nearby. She felt a little nervous as she
parked and went along to the enquiry desk, but it
seemed that Everard had warned the clerk that she was
coming, for after only a few minutes a tall very thin
young man in a white coat arrived, introduced himself
as the Professor's houseman, gave his name as Paul
van Vliet, cast her a look of the greatest admiration,
and offered to take her to Professor Herrisma.

His English was good, and by the time they had
gone down several corridors, up three floors in a lift
and along several more corridors, they were on a
firmly friendly base. But once in the Professor's office,
Paul became very correct and answered his chief with
great politeness, then made himself scarce before
Prudence could say another word.

As she shook hands with Everard she enquired: 'Is

he attached to you? Are you very strict or something? I expected him to click his heels and bow!'

Everard laughed. 'He's a good lad, just qualified and very keen; the young ones all tend to think of us consultants as hoary old despots. It's rather embarrassing at times.' He pushed forward a chair. 'Do sit down for a minute—did you have any difficulty getting here?'

'None—I drove Sibella to dancing class and then came on here and parked. I must fetch her in an hour, if that's all right with you? Aren't you busy?'

He smiled nicely at her. 'Well, yes, but I give myself an hour or so off when I can. Have you seen Benedict?'

'Here? No. Was I supposed to?'

'No, no—but he's got a teaching round this afternoon, I wondered if you had met him with his students.' He got up from his chair behind the desk. 'If you are ready, shall we start?'

Prudence had been in hospitals before, of course, but never behind the scenes. She peered into sterilizing rooms, dressing rooms, looked at nurses' duty stations and had the intercom explained to her, met several of the Ward Sisters and glimpsed the wards. The hour flew by and she enjoyed every minute of it. She said goodbye with regret and Everard walked with her to the entrance. 'I hope this will be the first of other meetings,' he told her. 'Perhaps at the weekend? Benedict tells me that you are free on Saturday afternoons and Sunday mornings.'

'That would be nice.' She meant it, but at the same time felt a pang of regret that it wasn't Benedict asking her. So silly, she told herself, getting into the car and waving cheerfully as she went. She was halfway across the courtyard when she was aware of Benedict standing near the gate, talking to two elderly men. He looked up as she passed and waved casually.

The days swept by. Prudence was well into her stride by now—on excellent terms with Sibella, accepted by the staff, even managing an odd word of Dutch now and then. Only with Benedict was she wary. When they had first met she had felt an instant liking for him and she had thought he too had felt the same about her, but now she wasn't so sure. He treated her in a calm and placid manner which left her at a loss to know if he liked her or not, and although she had every comfort she could have wished for, she soon discovered that she was expected to be ready to fit in with his work even if it meant typing letters in the late evening, sewing buttons on his shirts and driving round Appeldoorn with an important letter which had to be delivered without loss of time. Not that she minded, it was nice to feel that at last she was doing something useful.

She had lunch with the Brands on the Saturday, driving herself to their house on the other side of the town, and staying for the afternoon. And in the evening, feeling adventurous, she took herself to the cinema. She enjoyed the film—an English one with Dutch subtitles—but she didn't enjoy being on her own. She was used to men looking at her, her hair always attracted attention and she wasn't wearing a hat, but she had always had Tony with her before. Now she discovered that she was fair game. She shook off several hopeful hangers-on, got into her car and drove back to Benedict's house. Whatever else she did in the future, she wouldn't go to the cinema.

The house was quiet as she went into it through the garden door, but Ork popped his head round the kitchen door as she went along the passage to the front hall. 'You like dinner, Miss Prudence?' he asked.

She hesitated; she had eaten a cheese roll and drunk a cup of coffee after she had left the Brands' house, but that was hours ago. She shook her head reluctantly. Even kind old Ork couldn't be expected to find a hot meal for her at that hour. 'No, thank you, Ork.' She hoped her voice sounded as casual as she had tried to make it. 'I've had something . . .'

'A pity,' said Benedict from behind her. 'I've been out on a case and I'm famished. At least come and keep me company while I eat. Ork, I'm ready in five minutes.'

He swept her along with him into the hall and gave her a little push towards the staircase. 'Up with you and take off your coat, I'll be in the dining room.'

It was terrible when she got downstairs, the smell of hot soup sent her insides rumbling. She didn't think she'd be able to bear it. 'I'm sure you'd rather be on your own,' she began, with no success at all; she was sat in a chair beside Benedict and Ork ladled soup into a plate and set it before his master. Try as she might, she couldn't prevent a delicate sniff.

'You haven't had your dinner,' said Benedict blandly. 'Ork, bring another plate. Miss Prudence is going to have dinner as well.'

Prudence shot him a look. 'I don't want . . .' she began, and then as the plate was set before her: 'No, I haven't had dinner. I went to the cinema instead.'

'On your own?' His voice was gently enquiring.

'Well, yes.' She didn't look up from her plate.

'We'll have to do better than that, won't we?' He

turned round to speak to Ork and the old man went away and came back presently with a bottle of wine, then served them with spiced chicken with apricots. They had almost finished when Benedict said abruptly: 'I'm afraid the whooping cough epidemic is escalating. I've been called out to three cases this evening and there were double the number at the clinic this week.'

'Are they very ill—the children?'

'Some of them, yes. The thing is, have we enough staff to cope? It's a long illness. Mothers with other children won't be able to hold out, so the sick ones must go into hospital if it's possible.'

'So what do you do?'

He looked at her over his glass. 'Try and keep a step ahead.'

Prudence helped herself to the trifle Ork was offering. 'It's a silly question, but is there anything I can do?'

'Not at the moment—if there is I'll tell you. We'd better keep Sibella away from that dancing class for the time being—one of the children who goes to it fell ill this evening. We can let her go to school for the moment, she's in a small class and outside it she hasn't much contact with the other children. The children next door have all been inoculated, so she can go there to play and they can come here. Get her out for a good brisk walk each day and see that she eats properly.' He smiled suddenly at her. 'Let's have coffee in the drawing room.'

Ork brought the tray in after them and Prudence said urgently: 'I'll go and give Ork a hand clearing the table—it's so late . . .'

'You'll do no such thing—he'd be deeply offended

and suspect that we thought he was getting past his work. The three of them will make short work of the washing up. Now tell me, did you enjoy your lunch with the Brands?'

She enjoyed sitting there telling him about her afternoon, but she didn't stay long. On her way out of the room Benedict called after her. 'Take Sibella to church in the morning will you? I'll take Henry for his walk; I'll have to be away early and I probably shan't be in for lunch.'

She didn't see him again until the evening and then only briefly. There were to be clinics set up, he told her, so that all the babies and small children could be inoculated; it had to be organised and started straight away.

And Sunday set the pattern of the week, with glimpses of Benedict at one meal or the other, letters thrust at her with the request to answer them as best she might, the phone going almost unceasingly, and when Ork or Betje weren't there Prudence found herself coping as well as she was able. Nearly always the person the other end spoke some English, and she took careful note of their messages and phone numbers and left them on Benedict's desk where he would see them when he got in.

She cancelled her lunch date with the Pennicks and when Everard phoned put him off, regretfully, from inviting her out to dinner. 'We're a bit busy,' she explained, 'and although I can't help much, I am an extra pair of hands about the place.'

He had understood very nicely, they made a vague date for a week or so ahead and she hung up. She would have enjoyed an evening out; Benedict was still his usual placid self almost all the time, but once or

twice when something had gone wrong she had
glimpsed a well battened down rage and impatience.
He was looking tired, too, and although he was exactly
as he always was with his little daughter he had
snapped at Prudence once or twice, to apologise
immediately.

It was in the middle of the following week when he
came down to breakfast looking thunderous. He kissed
Sibella but his good morning to Prudence was very
terse. 'Prudence, I've got a job for you. When you've
taken Sibella to school I want you to go to my
consulting rooms—my receptionist has gone off sick
and I've no time to get a replacement. There's a nurse
there as well who speaks English, so do the best you
can.' He swallowed a cup of coffee, kissed his small
daughter once more and had gone.

Prudence gaped after him; she was prepared to
make allowances for him because he was bogged down
in a mass of extra work, but did he really think that
she could cope with a receptionist's job without any
warning whatsoever? A silly question, she told herself,
because presumably he did. Well, if he got all the
wrong patients and their names mixed up to boot, that
was his fault!

She took Sibella to school and drove to the address
he had given her, stopping to ask the way twice. By
the time she arrived in the narrow street with its row
of tall gabled houses, she was feeling belligerent. She
parked the car with a fine disregard for the board
telling her not to, and went up the narrow steps to the
door with Benedict's name on it. The first floor, he
had said. She pounded up the narrow stairs, so
annoyed that she quite forgot to feel any panic. The
landing was very small with three doors. She

examined them in turn and decided that 'Wachtkamer' was probably the safest. The second door had Dr van Vinke on it and he might be inside with a patient, the third door had Private, which was easily guessable.

The waiting room was surprisingly elegant, done out in a gentle grey and pale green with the merest hint of rose pink. Anyone feeling ill would doubtless feel better at the very sight of it, but Prudence had no time for that. There was a desk opposite the door, with no one sitting at it, and two people sitting in comfortable chairs looking uneasy.

Prudence muttered what she hoped was good morning, and crossed to the desk; there was a large sheet of paper on it with her name written large. Someone had written in capitals: 'Knock and come in when you get here.'

There was another door by the desk. She tapped briskly and went inside. Benedict was there, sitting beside an enormous desk writing. There were screens in one corner of the room and Prudence could hear voices. Nurse and patient, she guessed, and addressed herself to Benedict.

'I'm here,' she said baldly.

He glanced up at her. 'And in a towering rage,' he observed. 'Go into the third room on the landing and get into a white overall you'll find there. My receptionist isn't quite your shape,' he paused, eyeing her person, 'but you'll have to make do—pins or something. Then go to the desk where you'll find a pile of patients' notes and an appointments book—put the notes in order, will you, and then look at the names on the next page and take the notes for those patients out of the filing cabinet.' He nodded briefly and bent his head over his writing again.

Prudence didn't say a word. Without looking up he added: 'Stop seething and show a little of the British phlegm so deservedly admired. I did warn you that you'd be a general help.'

Prudence went out of the room, muttering to herself, found an overall in the small cloakroom leading off the landing and was instantly lost in its ample folds. She was by no means a skinny girl, but Benedict's receptionist must have been a size twenty at least. Luckily there was a belt; she gathered in as much as she could and went back to the waiting room.

There was another patient there now, but as she went in the nurse fetched the other two away. Prudence mumbled her version of good morning in Dutch and sat down at the desk. She found things exactly as Benedict had told her, and really it wasn't in the least difficult. She was at the filing cabinet getting out the next lot of patients' notes when the nurse came in again with her two patients. She smiled at Prudence. 'You will make an appointment for the first week in November?' she asked. 'English is spoken.'

She slid away with the next patient and two more came in. Prudence dealt with the elderly ladies who needed another appointment, ushered them out and bent a wary eye on the newcomers. They beamed back at her and spoke; it took her a few moments to discover that what they were saying was their name. Their card was on top of the small pile still on the desk. She uttered a relieved sigh and went back to the filing cabinet.

The morning wore on, and by twelve o'clock she was beginning to enjoy herself. But by then it was time to collect Sibella from school and the last of the patients had been ushered into Benedict's consulting room. It was the nurse who came out with the message that she should leave and that she wouldn't be needed again that day.

He could at least say thank you, thought Prudence, disentangling the overall and rushing down the stairs and into the car. Luckily there wasn't a great deal of traffic in the narrow side streets; she reached the school just as Sibella emerged.

There was no sign of Benedict at lunch. The two of them ate it alone and then with Henry for company went for their usual walk. It was turning colder and there was a mean wind blowing the leaves from the trees. They walked and ran and played tig with Henry obligingly joining in, and Sibella's small cheeks glowed. 'Papa is giving me a bicycle for Christmas,' she told Prudence as she danced along beside her. 'We will ride, you and me . . .'

'I,' corrected Prudence automatically. This was to be another of her duties, biking furiously round Appeldoorn, probably in the teeth of a nasty wind. 'Can you ride?' she asked.

Sibella gave her a limpid look. 'No, but you and Papa shall teach, is it not?'

Prudence explained about not saying 'is it not' and observed that Papa would teach her far better than anyone else.

Sibella nodded her small head. 'But of course, but you come too.'

Prudence smiled down at her; it was nice to be wanted. She thought with surprise that Benedict had wanted her too, although perhaps not in quite the same way.

Benedict didn't come home until she was putting Sibella to bed. He came into the bathroom where the

little girl was splashing around in the bath, and
Prudence was shocked at his tired face.

She asked urgently: 'Did you have lunch?'

He had gone to sit on the edge of the bath. 'No.'

'Tea, anything?'

'No, but don't fuss, Sitska's getting me a tray now.'

She lifted Sibella on to the bathmat and began to
dry her. 'You don't have to go out again, I hope?'

'I can't say. You did a good morning's work,
Prudence. Thank you.'

'I quite—I enjoyed it. I'm sorry I was ratty.'

He smiled tiredly. 'Whether you like it or not you'll
be doing it for several mornings—and by way of a
little light relief, one of the women helpers at the clinic
that's been set up has both her children ill with
whooping cough, so you'll have to go there three
evenings a week and help out.'

And at her look: 'It isn't going to last for ever, you
know.'

So the pattern of her days changed yet again, and
now she was busy from morning until bedtime, and
once she had got the hang of it, she coped very well.
The evening clinic was purely a matter of common
sense on her part and a capacity for hard work. There
was little need to speak, which was a good thing; her
work was mainly helping babies and small children out
of their coats, rolling up sleeves, drying tear-stained
little faces and ushering them and their mothers out
into the street again. There were several helpers to do
these mundane tasks, leaving the doctors and nurses
free for the more specialised work, and Prudence made
friends quickly.

Only when the last small patient had been wrapped up
and sent home and the work of clearing up began did she

begin to feel tired. It was bliss, when they were ready, to sit down and wait for Benedict to come from his office and walk her out to the Aston Martin. She sank back against the leather and wished the drive would last for hours instead of the ten minutes it took to get home. And once indoors, there was Ork ready with coffee and sandwiches arranged before the fire in the drawing room. When her three nights were done, she felt lost, watching Benedict leave the house, wishing she were going with him. As it was, she wasted her precious quiet evenings doing nothing, sitting in the lovely room following the evening's work in her mind's eye. Once on the first of these evenings she stayed up until he returned, only to be met by a look of irritation, quickly suppressed, and a demand as to why she hadn't gone to bed. She had made some excuse and said goodnight at once, and had taken care to be in her room before he came home on subsequent nights. She had made various excuses to herself about it, but deep down she was hurt. She had wanted to show him that she was concerned, even if she hadn't been working at the clinic, but she had merely annoyed him. She didn't know why—and come to that, she reminded herself crossly, she wasn't interested.

It couldn't last for ever, of course. At the end of the third week Benedict told her that things were on the mend; there was no need for her to go to the clinic any more. 'I shan't need to go either,' he added, 'and Mevrouw Palk will be back at my rooms in three days' time, so you'll be able to return to normal life.'

He told her over lunch, and Sibella, listening and understanding a good deal, piped up: 'Now I may have my Prudence for me again. I do not like it when she is not with me.'

Prudence beamed at the child, 'Now isn't that nice—I like being with you too. If your papa doesn't object, we'll think of something exciting to do together, just by way of a treat.'

Sibella wrinkled her small brow and Benedict translated the last part, then added in English: 'Aren't I invited?'

Sibella shrieked with joy. 'Yes, yes, Papa, it will be *geweldig*!'

'I think you mean splendid or something like that,' said Prudence. 'What do you want to do?'

Sibella got out of her chair and climbed on to her father's knee, put her arms round his neck and whispered. Benedict looked across to Prudence. 'It's a secret,' he said blandly. 'If you don't mind missing your free Saturday morning, we'll go then.' He was silent for a moment. 'That is unless you've made any dates?'

'Dates? Me? Mevrouw Penninck said she'd wait for a few weeks before making a date for lunch with her.' She was annoyed to feel her cheeks grow warm. 'And Everard Herrisma asked me to go to dinner, but I explained . . .'

'No doubt he will phone again. Have any evening you want, Prudence, after this week.'

'Are you going to marry Professor Herrisma?' asked Sibella. She said it in Dutch, but the meaning was clear enough.

'Certainly not,' said Prudence quickly, and added: 'Anyway, he hasn't asked me—you don't marry anyone unless he asks you first.'

All of which Benedict translated for Sibella, his face expressionless.

It was nice to return to her homely little chores each

day; have time to do the flowers and help with the delicate china and silver, take Henry for walks without having to rush back to get to the consulting rooms in time and type any letters for Benedict at a reasonable hour instead of dashing them off at any spare moment. And above all it was nice to have Benedict around the house more often. He didn't look tired any more either, although she surprised a thoughtful look on his handsome features from time to time as though he was worried about something—not quite worried perhaps, preoccupied was a better word. There had been no sign of Myra during the last busy week or two. Perhaps she was away or they had quarrelled, or perhaps she just didn't come to the house any more. Certainly Benedict had gone out in the evenings after dinner on one or two occasions since he no longer went to the clinic. Prudence told herself that she was becoming a nosey parker and turned her attention to the importance of what to wear on Saturday.

They left directly after breakfast, driving into a grey blustery morning, and when Benedict had turned on to the Amsterdam motorway, Prudence asked: 'Is that where we're going? Amsterdam?'

'How clever of you to guess. Sibella has decided that you must be shown the sights. We shall do the lot— museums, canal trip, royal palace, shops—in moderation, I hope—the Nieuwe Kerk, pausing from time to time for refreshment.' He glanced at Prudence. 'An unsophisticated day's outing.'

'It sounds super,' said Prudence, and meant it.

They had a hilarious day. Benedict parked the car, not an easy matter for the motorist in that city of canals and narrow streets, but since he was an honorary consultant at the largest hospital there, it was only a question of parking the Aston Martin in its forecourt and taking a taxi to the first item in their programme—the canal trip.

The day was a riotous success. Prudence was whisked from one thing to the other so that by the time they stopped for lunch she had a kind of kaleidoscope whirling around inside her head. They went to the Café du Centre at Dikker en Thijs, very elegant and, Prudence suspected, very expensive. Fortified by lobster patties, ravioli and an enormous ice cream, she was only too willing to be taken on a lightning tour of the shops and a slightly longer tour of the Rijksmuseum, not long enough, she declared, being hurried along to Madame Tussaud's Museum, a treat Sibella shrilly demanded Prudence should be allowed before they had tea.

They took a taxi from the Museum to the Amstel Hotel and had tea on the covered terrace and then had another taxi ride back to the hospital where the car was parked. It was dusk before they were home, racing down the motorway with a speed that Prudence found exhilarating. It was a terrible let-down to discover when they got back that Benedict was going out to dinner.

Perhaps it was because of her disappointment that she accepted Everard's invitation to have dinner with him on the following Wednesday. He phoned after dinner, as she was drinking her coffee in the drawing room, and perhaps she had been more eager than she had intended. It would be nice to have an evening out, and Everard was a nice man, but that was all. The remarks Benedict had made rankled still, and Prudence went to bed wondering if she should have refused or at least sounded a bit doubtful.

But Benedict showed no doubt at all when she told him. 'Go by all means! You deserve some fun after these last weeks, and Everard is a good companion.' He smiled at her with a casual good humour which for some reason annoyed her. 'Take a house key if you like.'

'I shan't be late,' she assured him stiffly.

It would have to be the blouse and skirt again, pretty enough for dining out, but perhaps she should write and ask her mother to send her something else, although there was nothing to stop her buying a dress. After all, she had spent almost nothing of her salary; she hadn't had the chance.

Everard came to fetch her and spent ten minutes or so talking to Benedict before they left the house, Everard driving a Mercedes with a regard for the rules of the road which annoyed her. She imagined that he would never exceed the speed limit on any account, which from her brief experience of driving in Holland was an unusual thing. All the same, he was a pleasant companion. He took her to the Peppermill in the town, a quiet restaurant now that the tourist season was over, and they dined unhurriedly, talking about everything under the sun. It was almost eleven o'clock when he drove her back, and the house, except for the porch lights and a glimmer from the hall lamps, was quiet and dark.

'Benedict out?' asked Everard. 'Well, it's more than likely. I won't come in. We must do this again, Prudence.'

She thanked him nicely, shook his hand before she sensed that given half a chance he would kiss her, and slipped indoors as Ork, in answer to her ring, let her in.

The house was warm and peaceful and lovely to come home to. She sighed and wished Ork a good evening, then started for the stairs. She had only taken a step or two when the study door was opened and Benedict came out.

'Back already? I hope you enjoyed your evening?'

'Very much, thank you.'

'The first of many?' Benedict's voice was faintly mocking and she bristled.

'I really don't know. In any case, I hardly expect to be free to go out just whenever I please.'

'Quite right. But of course, if you're genuinely fond of Everard . . .'

She goggled at him. 'Me? Fond of him? I hardly know him! He's a dear and I like him. You do jump to conclusions, don't you?'

'Perhaps.' His voice was cool and a little amused. 'He'd make a very good husband.'

'I daresay he would,' she snapped back at him. 'But it so happens that I don't particularly want to marry. Once bitten, twice shy, you know. I'm going to be very cautious next time. I certainly shan't do anything as silly as falling in love without very careful consideration first.'

His blue eyes danced with amusement, but he didn't smile. 'I agree with you; compatibility and friendship without heaving passion are much more likely to make a successful marriage, especially for us older ones.' He ignored the indignant sound· she made. He went on gently: 'I think it might be a good idea if you and I married on those terms, Prudence.' He turned back to the study. 'Give it some thought, will you? Goodnight.'

She felt she would explode with indignation. She

had had proposals before, but never one like that, offered casually and without waiting to find out what she thought about it. The arrogant wretch! In the morning she would give him a piece of her mind, pack her bags and go home. Temper took her upstairs to her room, where she flung off her clothes and jumped into bed, still seething. Indeed she actually got out again and started to pack a case, to stop in the middle because Sibella's little face danced before her eyes. She would leave, but not before she had concocted some suitable story to tell the little girl. They had grown fond of each other and it wasn't going to be easy to leave. A pity she wasn't fond of Benedict. She got back into bed, and went to sleep on a wave of indignation.

CHAPTER FIVE

PRUDENCE woke in the small hours and remembered with the clarity of thought which comes with the dead of night every word Benedict had said.

She sat up in bed, switched on her bedside light and pondered the matter. He had been joking; she dismissed the idea at once—Benedict wouldn't make that kind of joke. And just suppose he had been serious? She liked him, she enjoyed his company, she admired his ability to work hard, she trusted him. On the other hand, he could be arrogant when it suited him and she suspected that under that calm face he controlled a temper. Not that that worried her; she had a temper herself which she didn't always check . . .

She curled up against her pillows and fell into supposition, unlikely but interesting. She liked living in the old house; life was pleasant even if it was busy, and surely if she married him Benedict would see to it that someone would come and take over her chores? She had liked his friends—well, most of them, and she liked Appeldoorn and she had a genuine fondness for Sibella. Were those things enough to make a happy marriage? she wondered. He didn't love her; what was it he had said: 'Compatibility and friendship without heaving passion,' and, 'It would be a good idea if we married on those terms.'

She was a romantic girl; no way could she see any romance in his suggestion. It might not have been a joke, but he couldn't have been serious. She switched out the light and went back to sleep.

She overslept, which meant that she had to hurry in order to go down to breakfast with Sibella, and that left no time for thinking. Even if she had had time to get shy at meeting Benedict again, it wouldn't have mattered. There he was sitting at the breakfast table, looking as placid as he always did, wishing them good morning without a trace of awkwardness and then going back to his letters and newspaper. Presently he tossed some letters to her with the casual remark that she might answer them and have them ready for him to sign when he got home for lunch. 'There's nothing I need to dictate; I've scribbled a couple of dates down.' He got up kissed his daughter, nodded casually to Prudence and went out of the house.

He was home for lunch, came in for tea with them both and after a brief absence, back again for dinner, and not once did he attempt anything more than casual talk. It was on the tip of Prudence's forthright tongue to ask him just exactly what he had meant, but somehow the right moment never occurred. The day ended with his usual placid goodnight after dinner, a polite way of telling her that he didn't wish for her company.

'The man's mad!' declared Prudence, sitting before her mirror, brushing her fiery hair and frowning fiercely at her delightful reflection. He could explain himself on Doomsday as far as she was concerned. All the same, she admitted reluctantly, he was really rather nice; the way he came for tea at home, for instance, declaring that he was famished, tossing Sibella into the air, tickling her until she shrieked with laughter, romping with Henry; she forgot then that he could be remote and preoccupied and even terse, he was just a man coming home to his family and happy to do so.

She put the brush down slowly, still staring at her face. Would he come home to Myra in such a fashion? She doubted if that young woman would have her tea in the playroom or allow Henry to eat crumpets and loll in front of the fire. She would entertain elegantly in the drawing room and Benedict would be expected to join her and never mind Sibella. Myra would have an excellent governess for the little girl and see as little of her as possible.

'All guesswork,' Prudence informed her reflection, 'especially as I hate the girl. All the same, Sibella deserves a loving stepmother.'

She got up and wandered over to the bed and slid in. 'Like me,' she added at length, 'only it's an impossibility. I must have been having hallucinations or something.'

She had to eat her words on the very next day. She and Sibella had come in from their walk, glowing, a bit noisy and a little damp from the drizzle blown in all directions by the gusty wind. They were in the hall peeling off coats and scarves, discussing the advantages of buttered toast over jam sandwiches, when Benedict came out of his study. He looked them over with a faint smile, submitted to Sibella's hugs, begged her to take Henry to the kitchen to be dried, and only then turned to Prudence.

'Come into the study, Prudence.' He held the door open and after a moment's hesitation, she went.

'Is it urgent, Dr van Vinke?' she asked in a cool voice. 'Ork takes the tea tray up to the playroom,' she added pettishly. 'I don't like being ordered about.'

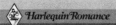
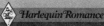

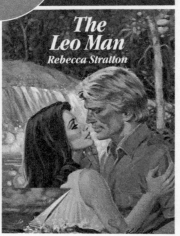

LOVE BEYOND REASON
There was a surprise in store for Amy!

Amy had thought nothing could be as perfect as the days she had shared with Vic Hoyt in New York City—before he took off for his Peace Corps assignment in Kenya.

Impulsively, Amy decided to follow. She was shocked to find Vic established in his new life...and interested in a new girl friend.

Amy faced a choice: be smart and go home...or stay and fight for the only man she would ever love.

MAN OF POWER
Sara took her role seriously

Although Sara had already planned her escape from the subservient position in which her father's death had placed her, Morgan Haldane's timely appearance had definitely made it easier.

All Morgan had asked in return was that she pose as his fiancée. He'd confessed to needing protection from his partner's wife, Louise, and part of Sara's job proved easy.

But unfortunately for Sara's heart, Morgan hadn't told her about Monique...

THE LEO MAN
"He's every bit as sexy as his father!"

Her grandmother thought that description would appeal to Rowan, but Rowan was determined to avoid any friendship with the arrogant James Fraser.

Aboard his luxury yacht, that wasn't easy. When they were all shipwrecked on a tropical island, it proved impossible.

And besides, if it weren't for James, none of them would be alive. Rowan was confused. Was it merely gratitude that she now felt for this strong and rugged man?

THE WINDS OF WINTER
She'd had so much— now she had nothing

Anne didn't dwell on it, but the pain was still with her—the double-edged pain of grief and rejection.

It had greatly altered her; Anne barely resembled the girl who four years earlier had left her husband, David. He probably wouldn't even recognize her—especially with another name.

Anne made up her mind. She just *had* to go to his house to discover if what she suspected was true...

Your Romantic Adventure Starts Here.

These FOUR free Harlequin Romance novels allow you to enter the world of romance, love and desire. As a member of the Harlequin Home Subscription Plan, you can continue to experience all the moods of love. You'll be inspired by moments so real. . .so moving. . .you won't want them to end. So start your own Harlequin Romance adventure by returning the reply card below. <u>DO IT TODAY!</u>

EXTRA BONUS
MAIL YOUR ORDER
TODAY AND GET A
FREE TOTE BAG
FROM HARLEQUIN.

He didn't answer at once, only smiled a little. 'Sit down, will you? And I've asked Ork to take Sibella to the kitchen for a few minutes, so you need not worry about her—tea will keep.'

He went and sat down behind the desk again, leaning back in his chair, his eyes on her face. 'Not a very romantic place in which to propose, is it?' he asked, and she could have sworn that he was laughing silently. 'But I don't think either of us feels that way. I thought if we had a sensible discussion and ironed out any differences . . .'

'You meant it the other evening?' She managed to keep her voice normal. 'I've had proposals before, but never one like that.'

'Ah, but the circumstances are rather different, aren't they? We are not bogged down in sentiment, we are able to talk about marriage unhampered by the wearing of rose-coloured spectacles.'

She glanced at him. He must be laughing, only he wasn't. His face wore its usual calm friendliness. She said weakly: 'What did you want to say?'

'I am aware that this is all a little unusual, but taking into account our circumstances, you must agree that it is also most sensible. I need a wife to run my home, sew buttons on my shirts, keep an eye on my appointments and entertain our friends, Sibella needs a mother desperately, and she already has a very strong affection for you. I am no longer very young—I shall be thirty-eight in a few months— and you are old enough to regard marriage as something more than swanning off into the sunset . . .'

Prudence gasped and muttered: 'I'm not that old!'

He agreed pleasantly. 'Indeed not, and when you're

racing around with Sibella you look ten years younger. Besides, you are a very pretty girl.' He fixed her with a bright blue eye. 'As I have already mentioned, we will leave the—er—romance out of it for the time being, such feelings have to grow without being urged. I think I am right in thinking that you've had your fill of falling in love for the time being. Time enough for that later on.'

'And supposing we don't ever—that is, if we just want to remain on a friendly basis?'

'Shall we cross that bridge when we get to it?'

She said hesitantly: 'I think marriage should be permanent, unless it's hopeless . . .'

'I agree.' He smiled. 'We agree about quite a lot of things, don't we?'

Prudence nodded, and then remembered something. 'What about Myra? I thought she was—well, your girl-friend.'

'Did you indeed?' His voice was silky. 'I can assure you that I don't have girl-friends. She happens to be someone whom I've known for some time—she was a friend of my wife's, but I've never had any desire to do more than take her out occasionally by way of a little light relief. Indeed, she isn't the only young woman I've dates with.' His eyes held hers for a long moment. 'If you will consent to be my wife you will be the only woman I shall date, Prudence.' He smiled slowly. 'Are there any more vexed questions?'

She shook her head, then said a little stiffly: 'I don't know anything about you.' She paused: 'I mean, your family and your—your wife . . .'

'My parents are dead, my wife was killed in an accident when Sibella was not quite a year old.' He said very evenly: 'She found life very dull being

married to a doctor; she liked parties and winter sports
and having fun. She was young—in her early twenties
—we had grown apart. I have lost count of the
people who have advised me to marry again, but
until I met you there was no one I could be
completely easy with. You fit into our lives so well,
Prudence, I believe that we could lead a contented
life, you and I and Sibella. But perhaps you would
become bored after a time.'

'Bored? How could I possibly be? There's always
something to do—Sibella and Henry, and of course
you . . .' She wasn't looking at him and missed the
amused gleam in his eyes. 'And there's Dutch to learn,
and your friends, and the shopping.'

'It sounds a little tedious. Life isn't always as
humdrum, though: there's no reason why you
shouldn't come with me when I go to England, and if
you do then of course Sibella can come too, and I
travel round quite a bit. Sibella and I ride—I don't
know if you do?' And when she nodded: 'I'll get you a
mount, there are some splendid stretches of country
not too far away.' He saw her face and added: 'Don't
decide now, tell your parents or Nancy if you wish,
ask their advice.'

'Suppose I refuse?'

'We'll go on as we are at present. Sibella is a lot
happier than she has been for months, Ork and Sitska
like you, my friends like you—for that matter, I like
you. I should want you to stay on as—well, what are
you? General assistant, Girl Friday, governess—I
wouldn't know.'

'You've forgotten the shorthand and the typing,'
Prudence reminded him. 'And I don't want to ask
anyone's advice. Funnily enough, the only person

whose advice I would take is yours. I'll sleep on it and tell you in the morning.'

Benedict nodded, got up and opened the door and when she was in the hall: 'Ask Ork to take up tea, will you? I'll be up in a few minutes.'

Prudence turned to look at him. He was smiling a little, his voice had been casual and placid as though they had nothing more on their minds than some small household problem.

What was more, neither by word or look did he so much as hint as to their conversation. They had tea, played cars with Sibella, and presently met downstairs before dinner, over which meal they discussed the various types of schooling he had in mind for Sibella. It was all a little frustrating, thought Prudence, going up to bed after a suitable interval, leaving her to decide such an important matter by herself. After all, he would be as involved as she. That this was quite illogical didn't enter her head, and in any case she was aware in her heart that her mind was already made up. She would marry him; not for love but certainly for liking and because she wanted to live in the lovely old house and share his interests, in the same way as friends shared. He was quite right, falling in love was no great shakes, one only fell out again or got taken for granted, just as Tony had taken her for granted. She would be content and quietly happy, and it would be fun to watch Sibella grow up.

She undressed and before she got into bed, went along to see that the child was asleep. Sibella was curled into a tight ball in her small bed, and Henry was sprawled untidily across its foot. He opened an eye and wagged his tail, he would go for his run in the garden with Benedict and sleep in his basket at the back of the hall. She kissed Sibella, tweaked Henry's ear, and padded back to her own room.

Lying wakeful, she reflected that the expression 'to sleep on it' was a load of nonsense. Whoever slept soundly on a problem needed their head examined!

But it was obvious the next morning that Benedict had no problems. His 'good morning' was uttered with calm. The colossal conceit of the man! thought Prudence, suffering from lack of sleep. Her own greeting was on the snappy side and she barely glanced at him, aware at the same time that her bad temper was at variance with the fact that she had made up her mind to marry him. She was halfway through her first cup of coffee when he said: 'Sibella, will you go to my bedroom and fetch my pocket book? I've left it on the tallboy. You'll have to stand on a chair to reach it, so be careful.'

Sibella skipped off, they could hear her feet pattering across the hall and running up the staircase. 'Well?' asked Benedict. 'You wanted to sleep on it, but I can see that you've been awake for most of the night.'

'Yes, I have.' She threw him a peevish look.

'Quite unnecessary. I slept soundly.' He sounded so smug that she could have thrown something at him.

'Not worth thinking about, I suppose,' and then her ill temper collapsed at his gentle: 'I had already done all my thinking, Prudence. I had no problem. I've asked you to marry me and I hope that you will say yes.'

Small feet were scampering downstairs. 'Well, I will,' said Prudence. There was no time to say more, because Sibella came dancing into the room.

'Just in time for some good news,' declared her father, and lapsed into Dutch.

Sibella had been standing by his chair; now she capered round to Prudence and flung herself at her. 'Nice, very nice! Now you are Mama!' She leaned up and kissed Prudence, then ran back to her father to fling her arms round his neck.

He smiled at Prudence over the small head. 'We must talk, but not now. This evening, I think. Now I must come down to earth and go to work.' He kissed Sibella and got up and started for the door, but turned back after a few steps, bent over Prudence's chair and kissed her.

'I'm entitled to do that now, aren't I?' he said softly. '*Tot ziens.*'

Prudence set about her usual morning's routine. She hadn't meant to say anything to Benedict until the right moment, certainly not in two minutes flat in the middle of breakfast. But it was done now, and she had to admit that she felt pleasantly elated and just for the time being she was content to busy herself with her chores and let future plans take care of themselves. And since Benedict didn't come home for lunch there was no need to put any of her thoughts into words. In any case, the thoughts were chaotic and she would have been hard put to it to make herself clear. It was Sibella who did the talking, rattling on in her strange mixture of Dutch and English, making plans for a wedding, Christmas, a holiday next year, as well as stating her wishes about new clothes for these events.

'It's a bit early,' protested Prudence.

'You will marry now, this week?' demanded the little girl.

'Well, no. You see, it takes a little time—papers and things, and I'll need a dress to be married in . . .'

Sibella liked the idea of white satin, a train, an

enormous veil and a bunch of bridesmaids. 'And I will be a bridesmaid,' she declared.

'No, love—you see, I think we shall have a very quiet wedding, no bridesmaids and just a few people there. I'll certainly not wear white satin.' To clinch the argument Prudence added: 'I'm too old. When you grow up and get married you shall have white satin.'

A red herring which kept Sibella happily occupied for the rest of the afternoon.

They were just finishing tea when Benedict came in, and Sibella fell upon him at once, arguing hotly in favour of an enormous wedding. He listened patiently, translating for Prudence, and when the small voice had at length petered out:

'Well, if we do all that, it'll take at least six months to get ready, so Prudence can't be your mama until next summer.' He looked at Prudence. 'But perhaps you would like it that way?'

She said no so hastily that he smiled, then began to talk to Sibella again. The child listened carefully, then nodded her head. 'I've suggested that there's an alternative,' he told Prudence. 'We'll go shopping and buy you a splendid dress and give a party for all our friends. When we are married, of course.'

'That sounds fun. You do understand don't you. I mean me wearing white satin . . .'

'Yes, of course. We'll discuss the details later when this bossy boots has gone to bed. How about a game of Snakes and Ladders?'

It wasn't until after dinner that they had a chance to talk. Ork had been given the good news earlier in the day and they had had to suffer his benign glances as he served dinner—a special one, he informed them, by way of celebration.

'And that makes me feel mean,' observed Benedict. 'I should have taken you out, shouldn't I, to celebrate.' He said something to Ork, who hurried away. 'I've tried to make amends by telling him to get some champagne up from the cellar.'

'I'd rather be here,' said Prudence, and meant it.

They had their coffee in the drawing room and Prudence, nicely elevated by champagne, listened to Benedict's calm voice proposing this and that, and found herself agreeing to all he said. A quiet wedding as soon as possible, and from her home, an announcement to be put in the papers at once, no honeymoon, for the simple reason that he had more work than he could cope with for the next month or so, and lastly her return to Little Amwell.

'I suppose I must go?' she asked.

'Having you in my employ under my roof is one thing, to harbour you as my fiancée is quite another—yes, you must go. Perhaps we might phone your father presently and ask him to find out the best way to get a special licence. I shouldn't think it would take more than a few days, in which case you can go home at the end of the week and Sibella and I will come over for the wedding. I must warn you that I'm up to my eyes in work, so we'll have to come straight back here on the same day.'

'That's fine. It'll give me a chance to get some winter clothes. Do we have to have a best man and so on?'

'I'll bring Everard, and if I may my godmother. I told her today, by the way, and we're to go to dinner tomorrow evening.'

'I've no clothes,' said Prudence. 'Some blouses and a skirt are all I bought.'

He smiled faintly. 'We'll take a day together as soon as possible and settle that question. In the meantime I don't think Mevrouw van der Culp is going to mind what you wear. You always look very nice.'

She said uncertainly: 'You do think we're doing the right thing, don't you?'

His calmness reassured her. 'Yes, I do. I believe we shall be very content together.' He was watching her carefully from under lazy lids. 'You have no regrets about Tony? There's always the possibility that you will meet again some day.'

'I haven't thought about him for weeks,' said Prudence. 'Isn't it awful to think that if I hadn't spoken to you at Nancy's wedding I might still be waiting to marry him?' She added with a sudden flash of panic. 'You don't think I'm flighty, do you?'

He answered her gravely. 'No, Prudence, I don't. On the contrary, you have a most stabilizing influence on me.'

'Oh, well, that's good.' She glanced at the clock. 'I'd better go to bed, I expect you've got work to do.'

But as she got to her feet he stood up too. 'I almost forgot.' He fished around in his pocket and produced a little box. 'Your engagement ring. It's been in the family for a long time and it seems to me that it would suit you.'

Prudence took the box and opened it. The ring inside was very beautiful, a large diamond set in a cluster of smaller stones, mounted in an old fashioned gold setting.

'It's magnificent.' She looked at him. 'Suppose it doesn't fit?'

For answer he took the ring from her and slipped it on her finger. 'A good omen?' he suggested, and bent to kiss her cheek. 'Goodnight, Prudence. I'll see about your tickets tomorrow and we'll phone your father after breakfast.'

She stood at her window, looking out on to the garden below for quite some time. It was raining a little and windy, but the house was solid and warm all round her. 'It's home,' she told herself happily; she never wanted to live anywhere else, she was so content. Perhaps to be content was more important than being in love.

She telephoned her home directly after breakfast, before Benedict left the house. She was answered by her mother. 'Darling, you're not ill—is anything the matter? You don't usually phone . . .'

'Everything's fine, Mother. Benedict wants to speak to Father. We're going to be married.'

She listened to her mother's spate of excited questions. 'Look, love, I'll phone you later and we'll have a good gossip, but could you get Father now? Benedict has to leave in a few minutes and he's very busy.'

She handed the phone over and sat on the edge of the desk listening to his placid voice asking matter-of-fact questions. Presently he handed the phone back to her. 'That's settled,' he observed. 'I must go, I expect you'd like a word.'

He smiled at her and went out of the room. He hadn't kissed her, but perhaps that was a habit he didn't intend to make. She must remember not to expect it. She talked to her father, answering his sensible, fatherly questions, arranged to phone later in the day and went to get Sibella ready for school. A day like any other, only she was wearing a ring on her finger.

She dressed carefully that evening, wishing she had something more elegant in which to visit Mevrouw van der Culp, but Benedict's, 'Very nice,' as she joined him in the hall did much to restore her ego and the old lady's kindly, 'You are just right for Benedict, and so elegant, my dear,' made her evening.

Mevrouw van der Culp had a charming house—too large, as she pointed out to Prudence, but she was too old to change now. They had drinks in a drawing room furnished with a profusion of overstuffed chairs, small tables and standard lamps, but a fire blazed in the hearth and the room had a lived-in air and suited the owner. The dining room was small in comparison, all dark oak and red velvet, but dinner was superb, served on white linen with gleaming silver and delicate china. Mevrouw van der Culp made no secret of her satisfaction at their news. 'I've made no secret of my wish to see you married, Benedict,' she told him. 'I hope I'm to be invited to the wedding. When is it to be?'

'Yes, of course you are coming—it will be soon. Prudence goes home on Saturday and Sibella and I will follow as soon as I can arrange for someone to take over for a couple of days. Everard is to be best man. It's to be very quiet. Prudence's father will marry us from her home.'

The old lady nodded. 'I'm sure Everard is delighted.' She turned a faded blue eye on Prudence. 'He was greatly attracted to you, my dear.'

Prudence returned the look with a pleasant smile. 'He's a nice person, isn't he? We had dinner together a week or so ago—I shall value his friendship.'

Her hostess beamed at her and nodded again. 'Yes, you will be a good wife to Benedict. You're wearing the Vinke ring, I see. Doria—his first wife—disliked the family jewels, her ring was platinum, I remember, with a great topaz.'

Prudence peeped at Benedict, but his face was inscrutable; if he minded Mevrouw van der Culp talking about his first wife, he gave no sign.

They stayed talking for a long time and when they got back Benedict said kindly: 'Do you want anything? No? Then go to bed, my dear. I've some reports to read.'

She wished him a cheerful goodnight, made some lighthearted comment upon their evening and ran upstairs, holding back disappointment. Even friends kissed occasionally.

She was halfway up when he overtook her. 'It would be a thundering lie if I told you I was quite out of the habit of kissing girls, but I still have to get into the habit—a delightful one—of kissing you, Prudence.'

His kiss was quite something this time. She found herself looking forward to the next one.

Benedict drove them to Schiphol, Sibella between them. The matter of the special licence had been dealt with, and they were to be married on the following Wednesday, which gave her almost no time at all to find something to wear for the wedding. There's that nice place in Sherborne,' she mused. We could drive over, or Taunton . . .

'You're very quiet,' said Benedict. 'Cold feet?'

'Certainly not! I'm trying to think of somewhere where I can find an outfit. I will not be married in a Jaeger suit!' She added: 'There really wasn't any time to find anything in Appeldoorn, though I'm glad Sibella's got something pretty.'

He threw her a quick amused glance. 'I'm sure

you'll look charming whatever you wear.'

She felt quite lost once they'd said goodbye, and she had gone through Customs and Passport control. Wednesday seemed a long way off, and she had got so used to a way of life with Benedict and Sibella and the rest of the household. She accepted the coffee she was offered and watched Holland's coast slide away into the grey horizon.

Nancy met her at the airport, bubbling over with questions, full of advice, saying a little smugly that she had felt in her bones that Prudence and Benedict would hit it off. 'What are you wearing?' She wanted to know. The subject kept them busy for the whole of the drive to Little Amwell.

Her mother was just as excited, although she said rather longingly: 'It's such a pity that you can't have a pretty wedding like Nancy, darling.'

'Mother, I don't mind,' Prudence reassured her parent for the tenth time. 'We wanted a quiet affair, and anyway there would be no time—we have to go back to Appeldoorn in the afternoon, Benedict's got some conference or other he simply can't miss.'

'Is he a very busy man, darling?'

She thought of her solitary dinners. 'Yes, very.'

'Well, I must say it's all very sudden,' began Mrs Trent, intent on worming out as much as possible without appearing to do so. 'You haven't been there very long . . .'

'No, but you forget we see each other every day. Benedict's very much a family man . . .' She wished she hadn't said that, for her mother's eye brightened.

'How nice, darling,' she murmured. 'I've always wanted to be a granny—they can come and stay in the school holidays.'

Prudence's lovely eyes lost their sparkle. 'Something to look forward to, Mother dear.'

Wednesday was upon them before they knew where they were. Prudence and Nancy had driven to Sherborne and searched the few boutiques there and found a smoky grey dress with a matching quilted jacket and a little hat with a sweeping bunch of satin ribbons jauntily at the back. Shoes and bag and gloves, undies and make-up, and Prudence professed herself satisfied.

'Anyway, Benedict's loaded, isn't he?' observed Nancy. 'James says he's more or less a millionaire.' She glanced at Prudence's astonished face. 'Didn't you know? Probably not, he's not one to air his private affairs. Nice for you, love!'

It quite upset Mrs Trent when Benedict came knocking on the door an hour before they were due to go to church. 'You can't see her,' she said agitatedly. 'It's not lucky.'

It was Mabel who led him upstairs to Prudence's room, flung open the door and cried: 'Here's your intended, Miss Prudence—your ma wasn't liking the idea of him seeing you before you were wed, but maybe you've got something to talk about at the last minute.'

Prudence swung round from the dressing table. 'Oh, Mabel, thank you, you are a darling!' Her eyes slid past the devoted prop of the Trent household and fastened on Benedict. He always dressed well, but this morning he looked the epitome of elegance—dark grey suit, silk shirt, Gucci tie. He dropped a kiss on Mabel's cheek and crossed the room, laid the flowers on the dressing table and bent and kissed her. Mabel, lingering at the slowly closing door, watched and went

downstairs to report that the bridegroom was a
smasher and kissing the bride with a satisfying degree
of enthusiasm.

Mrs Trent wiped away a tear. 'Oh, Mabel, I'm so
happy! I began to think—you know, when Prudence
broke off with Tony—but now it's going to be all
right.'

Sentiments shared by her daughter as she sailed
down the aisle on an uncle's arm to where Benedict,
with Everard beside him, was waiting for her. He
turned and looked at her as she reached his side and
she wondered if he was remembering that they had
met on that very spot not so long ago. He must have
done, because he smiled at her, a secret smile, just for
her alone.

There was only a handful of guests, with Mevrouw
van der Gulp in a hat which vied with her mother's
and Sibella in her new velvet coat and beret, but the
church was full all the same. The village had turned
out to a man; Prudence was popular and they
wished her well—the women wanted to see what she
was wearing and admire the bridegroom. Besides,
there was nothing much doing until Christmas; now
there would be something to talk about for days to
come.

There was a sit-down lunch after the ceremony
before Prudence changed into the Jaeger suit, bade
everyone farewell and got into the car with Benedict.
It surprised her to find that Sibella was to travel
back with Everard and Mevrouw van der Culp, and as
they left the village behind them she remarked on
it.

She wouldn't admit disappointment when he said
matter-of-factly: 'Well, there are one or two things to

discuss, I thought it would be a good opportunity to get them settled on our own.'

He sent the car racing ahead and they sat in companionable silence for a bit. 'We've never talked about money,' he said presently. 'I've got plenty . . .'

Prudence interrupted him. 'I meant to have asked you when you came to my room, but somehow I forgot. Benedict, Nancy says you're almost a millionaire! I didn't know, truly I didn't—I mean, I haven't married you for your money. In fact, if I had known I might not have married you.'

'I imagined that, that's why I didn't tell you.' She felt his great shoulders shake with laughter. 'Don't be a goose about it, Prudence. You must take over the household money when we get home. Sitska will expect that. I deal with the big bills and you'll have an allowance, both for Sibella and yourself. Now that I have a wife, we must do some entertaining. I've a number of friends and any number of acquaintances. Then there is my work—I'll explain that to you in detail; there's my private practice, the clinic where I work several times a week, and the hospital. I lecture in Holland and I come to England frequently. If it doesn't interfere with Sibella's schooling, you'll come with me. I think perhaps we must have more help in the house.' He gave her a laughing sidelong glance. 'You must have the leisure to have coffee with your friends, go shopping, knit . . . whatever it is women do when they're at home.'

'I'm not very good at knitting,' observed Prudence meekly, 'but if you like the idea I'll get some wool and needles.'

He laughed at that, and they whiled away the rest of the journey talking about the wedding. The skies had clouded over by the time they reached the Hovercraft in mid-afternoon, and an early dusk was creeping round them.

There weren't many cars, and they were going on board when Prudence saw Everard's car behind them. They joined up during the crossing, but once on the other side, the Aston Martin raced ahead. They were home before the others. Prudence had had time to tidy herself, admire the buffet supper Sitska had laid out in the dining room and look at the cards waiting for them. When Everard's car stopped before the door, Benedict took her arm. 'Come and welcome your guests, my dear,' he told her, 'into your home.'

CHAPTER SIX

THE touch of Benedict's hand on her arm sent a thrill of pleasure through her; the day had been so full, so much had happened in it that she hadn't quite realised until that moment that she was really his wife. She had listened to Ork and Sitska and Betje offering congratulations, been led upstairs by Sitska and shown into a vast bedroom in the front of the house, surprised to find her cases in it, and gone back downstairs to Benedict, but before she could utter a word, they were standing in the porch, side by side. She was Mevrouw van Vinke now, and this was her home.

Sibella came tumbling out of the car, huge eyes in a small tired face, talking excitedly. She kissed them both and ran inside to find Sitska, while Everard helped Mevrouw van der Culp into the house.

'We stay only a very short time,' declared the old lady. 'You should be alone, the two of you. You make a very handsome couple, you know. I shall look forward to dining here, but not just yet.'

Benedict took her arm. 'Sitska has laid out supper for us all—we mustn't disappoint her, and I for one am famished!'

He led the old lady into the dining room and Prudence followed with Everard. There was a splendid buffet supper set out for them and Prudence said: 'Oh, I must fetch Sibella; she must have something before she goes to bed. What a gorgeous spread—whose idea was it?'

Benedict smiled. 'It seemed to me that we'd have to do something to mark the occasion; there wasn't much time at your place. We'll give a party to celebrate, but this will have to do for the moment.'

'But it's super!' She beamed her gratitude at him, then gave a little gasp as Sibella came carefully into the room, carrying a small wedding cake. There had been a wedding cake at the reception, of course, but this was rather special. Prudence looked across at Benedict, her lovely eyes sparkling. 'Benedict, how kind of you! I can't imagine a nicer way to end the day.' She smiled rather tremulously, and he said:

'Come over here, my dear, and cut the cake.'

They stood side by side, cutting the cake together with Ork and Sitska and Betje there too, and presently they drank more champagne and finally the party broke up. Sibella was very tired by now, she bade everyone goodnight and Prudence, excusing herself on the plea of getting the child to bed, said goodbye to her guests at the same time, and went upstairs with her. By the time she went down again the house was quiet, the remains of the party had been cleared away and Benedict was sitting in his chair, reading his letters.

He got up when she went in, pulled a small easy chair to the fire and begged her to make herself comfortable. 'But if you're tired,' he suggested kindly, 'do go to bed. Have you everything you want?'

She nodded. 'I'm in another bedroom . . . a very beautiful room . . .'

He raised his eyes briefly from the letter he was reading. 'It was my mother's, I'm glad you like it.' He smiled suddenly. 'I feel as though we have been married for a long time. That's a compliment, by the way.'

Prudence smiled and murmured 'Thank you.' She rather shared that feeling too; it didn't seem in the least strange, sitting here on the opposite of the fireplace, just keeping him company. She would really have to get some embroidery or tapestry work or, better still, a Dutch phrase book. Neither of these being at hand, she picked up a copy of *The Lancet* and began to read. Parts of it were rather off-putting, but on the whole it was quite absorbing. Benedict's amused voice cut short her study of something called Pacini's corpuscles.

'I didn't know you were interested in my work, Prudence.'

She reminded him with some dignity: 'I've got my First Aid badge, you know,' and waited while he roared with laughter. 'What is a Pacini corpuscle?'

'Well now, that's perhaps a little difficult to explain, they're receptors in the deeper connective tissue of the skin, they register vibration and pressure . . . Are you really interested, Prudence?'

'Oh, yes. I'd like to know a lot more about your work, so that when you come home and perhaps want to talk about it, I'll be able to understand.' She smiled a little. 'And make intelligent comments.'

Benedict stared at her thoughtfully. 'You know, I've missed that, someone to talk to—and I don't mean social chat, just someone to listen.'

'But you work in the evenings, don't you?'

'Yes, but only because it gives me something to do. Even when I am working it will be nice to have someone sitting there, just to look at from time to time.'

Prudence took a good look at him, sitting there in a muddle of envelopes and paper. It struck her that he must have been lonely since his first wife's death. Oh, there were always girls to take out for an evening, but she quite understood that that wasn't the same as going home to your own fireside with a willing listener to absorb your grumbles and comments about the day's work. And I'll be a willing listener, she promised silently, and a good wife, seeing that your house is run as you like it, and welcoming your friends and loving little Sibella, and being a friend too.

'If you've finished the letters, will you tell me about your day's work so that I know exactly . . .' she began.

Benedict put down the last of the letters. 'Each day's different; you'll be a great help jotting down reminders on my desk—there's always a notebook there. I'll leave you phone numbers so that you can reach me if you should need to and we can plan my free time together so that we make the most of it. Now this is my day, more or less . . .'

He told her very precisely so that by the time he had finished she had a good idea of his routine.

'But you're not always free on a Sunday?'

'I'm now on call every third weekend, which means that we can go out and about as long as there is a phone close by and I'm not more than twenty minutes or so away from the hospital.'

'And at night?'

'Well, I'm only called if it's really urgent. My registrar is a good man, he copes with almost all the cases at hospital, but I'm always available. I can be called to private patients at night, of course, and often am.' He gave her a questioning look. 'Do you suppose you'll be able to cope with delayed meals, broken dates and a bad-tempered husband when he's been out all night?'

'Of course I can. And we're so lucky, we've got Ork and Sitska and Betje, haven't we?' She glanced at him so briefly that she missed the sudden gleam in his eyes. 'And at least I do come from a household where there was a good deal of coming and going at awkward hours.'

Benedict said quietly: 'I believe we are going to have a very pleasant life together, Prudence.'

She smiled widely at him. 'So do I. Do you want to work now? I've delayed you . . .'

'Not tonight—everything has happened so quickly it's rather nice to have a breathing space.' He got up and pulled the old-fashioned bell rope. 'Let's have some coffee, shall we?'

So they sat and talked, quiet talk about the house and Sibella and his friends, so that Prudence felt, by the time she got reluctantly to her feet, that she really was Mevrouw van Vinke, about to embark on a pleasant married life. And Benedict's light kiss as she wished him goodnight clinched the matter.

He was, she decided, as she got ready for bed, the very nicest person she had ever met; she felt as though she had known him all her life. So it was possible to like a man very much without being in love with him—Nancy and she had argued about that years ago, when they were in their teens and full of ideas. She wandered about the lovely room, admiring the mahogany fourposter, the elegant tallboy and the Pembroke table between the windows with its triple mirror and silver candlesticks. There was a great gilded mirror on one wall and facing it a pillow cupboard, and under the mirror a steel fireplace with a small fire burning and a little buttonback chair drawn up to it. There were flowers too, and pale apricot-shaded lamps. Presently when she had had her bath, she wandered across to the Empire sofa and sat down on it to brush her hair. The sofa was upholstered in striped apricot silk and was in the Grecian style; Prudence decided then and there that she would find a dressing gown to match, and presently, nicely tired, still thinking about the clothes she would buy, she climbed into bed and closed her eyes. 'My wedding day,' she told the room. 'Not quite like most, perhaps, but I'm happier than I've been for a long time. I wonder why?'

Naturally there was no answer; she went to sleep.

She woke early. The morning's routine would be the same as any other, she supposed, but in this she was wrong, for hard on the heels of Betje with her morning tea came Sibella, to climb into bed beside her, sip tea from her cup and chatter. 'I have seen Papa,' she told Prudence. 'Always I go to say good morning to him when I wake, and then I say it again when I go downstairs. Now I shall do it for you also.'

'How very nice,' said Prudence, and meant it. They emptied the tea pot between them before the little girl went away to get dressed, leaving Prudence to shower and dress quickly and go along to the child's room to brush her hair and tie her shoelaces. That done, they went downstairs together and found Benedict already there, eating his breakfast and reading his letters.

He got up, kissed his daughter and then kissed Prudence with a placid: 'Good morning, my dear,' and smiled at them both. 'I'm in a hurry, I'm afraid, Prudence, go through the letters for me will you? If you can sort them out it would be a great help. I'll be home for lunch. Have a nice morning?'

He had gone, and the room seemed empty without

him. The pair of them ate their own breakfast, taking too long over it because they talked about the wedding, so that they had to hurry to school through the blustery autumn morning.

'I'll be here at twelve o'clock,' said Prudence, and bent to kiss the little face. 'We'll take Henry for a long walk after lunch. Be good.'

Sibella beamed at her. '*Tot ziens*, Mama.' She scampered off and Prudence watched her disappear inside the school entrance before she started back home. Once there, she went along to the little room where she had worked and began to sort the letters. There were quite a few; she puzzled out the bills and circulars and set them on one side, made a little pile of the letters, then read the two from England. The first asked Benedict to give a lecture in Bristol in six weeks' time, the second was from a doctor in London, asking for the notes of a patient Benedict had seen while she was staying in Holland. Prudence, hoping that she was doing the right thing, looked through the filing cabinet against one wall, found the notes and put them with the letter. Perhaps she was overreaching herself, but Dr Baxter's wife in the village at home always did the paper work for him; she presumed that most doctors' wives did. Anyway, if he didn't want her to do so, he could tell her.

He was pleased and a little surprised, and she felt a glow of pleasure when he thanked her. 'But you don't have to do this, you know,' he observed, 'although I must say it is very nice for me.' He laughed at her gently. 'You're a lady of leisure now, whatever that means. Do you suppose we should get someone to help with Sibella? Take her off your hands?'

Prudence looked at him in horror. 'Heavens, no!

She's no trouble, and we have such fun together—besides, what would I do all day? I've got quite quick with my typing and I'm beginning to find my way around the shops and understand what Sitska says. And walking in the afternoon with Sibella and Henry is such fun.'

'Don't you want to shop? For clothes, I mean. Which reminds me, I've opened an account for you at my bank. I'll take a couple of hours off tomorrow and we'll go there together. I'm free this next Saturday, we'll go to Arnhem, the three of us, and do some shopping then.'

Her eyes sparkled. 'Oh, Benedict, how super!'

'Yes—well, I must get back to work. I'll be home for tea, but I'll have to pay a couple of visits before dinner.'

He didn't kiss her this time, and she felt disappointed.

It was chilly outside; they came racing in from their walk, tidied themselves quickly and joined Henry in front of the playroom fire. Benedict was due at any moment. Prudence found herself listening for his tread on the stairs and turned to smile at him when he came in. He stood by the door for a moment, a look on his face she couldn't understand, then bent to swing Sibella into the air before sitting down by the fire.

'I saw Ork in the hall, tea's on the way,' he told her. 'Did you have a good walk?'

'Lovely! Henry's exhausted—he goes twice as far as we do, of course.'

'We'll take him for a run on Sunday morning before church—all three of us. We missed you, did you know?'

Her green eyes met his steady blue ones. 'No, I didn't. I'd love to come with you.'

Ork came in then with the tea and she poured for them all and handed round buttered toast, sitting back on her heels like a small girl with Sibella beside her. 'Why do you have a nice old-fashioned English tea?' she asked. 'Mevrouw Brand said they only drank tea and ate a biscuit.'

'Because of Sibella, I suppose. It gave me a chance to see something of her, and children love teatime, don't they?'

'I do too, don't you? Not the food only, but sitting there like this . . .'

'I find it delightful.' Benedict spoke quietly, his eyes on her down-bent head.

They took Sibella to school before going to the bank in the morning. Prudence sat in the manager's office, trying to understand what was being said; true, Benedict did explain something to her from time to time, but she suspected that a lot more was being discussed than she was being told about. Finally she was given a cheque book and told that her first quarter's allowance was in the bank and that she could take out what she wanted.

'It's almost exactly like your own bank in England,' said Benedict, 'but you might as well have a go while we are both here.'

'Yes, all right, but I've still some money of my own.' She caught his eye and didn't go on, because he looked suddenly annoyed. But all he said softly was: 'My money is yours now, my dear.'

'How much?' she asked. 'I used about a hundred gulden a week before—before we married.'

'You'll need more than that. Divide your allowance into thirteen if you like and then you'll know roughly how much you can spend in a week.' He told her how much that was, and she gasped.

'But, Benedict, that's far too much! Whatever shall I do with . . .'

'Exactly what you like.' His placid voice had become suddenly obdurate. 'And please don't argue, Prudence.'

So she meekly did as she was told and accompanied him outside into the street. Once clear of the doors, she stopped and looked at him. 'I've annoyed you. I'm sorry, but you do seem to have rather a lot of money and I'll have to get used to it. I've never been exactly poor, but I'm a bit out of my depth.'

He looked at her unsmilingly. 'I've no intention of a little thing like money coming between us. We stand on a most agreeable footing—let us remain so, shall we?'

She smiled then. 'Oh, yes, Benedict. That's the best of being on such good terms, isn't it? We can speak our minds like old friends and not take umbrage.' He glanced at his watch and she said at once: 'I expect you want to go to your rooms—or is it the hospital? Thank you for coming with me. Will you be home for lunch?'

His firm mouth twitched. 'The hospital,' he told her. 'But not just yet, and I'll be home for lunch. Let's get some coffee somewhere—there's a place just across the street.'

He tucked a hand under her arm and together they crossed the street.

'What are you doing this morning?' he wanted to know.

'I've got to get some flowers and I promised I'd get some salad for Sitska, to save her or Betje going out later, and I want some buttons for Sibella's red dress—she's lost two—and something to work at in the evening's, and some stamps.' She broke off. 'What a dull recital compared with your morning!'

Benedict shook his head. 'No, it's not. It's soothing; half way through some medical tangle I shall think of you carefully matching red buttons and the world will seem right again.'

She opened her eyes wide at that. 'Really, what a nice thing to say! I shall think about you too, not all the time, of course, but now and then.'

She poured the coffee and passed him a cup. 'Sibella was chattering away about Sint Nicolaas when I was putting her to bed yesterday—surely that's in December?'

'It is, but it's rather an occasion for the small children. We must find out what she wants. I promised her a bike for Christmas, so we'll have to think of something else. A doll?'

'If I could find a nice old-fashioned one. I'll dress it and perhaps we could find a cot . . .'

Half an hour had gone in a flash. Benedict signalled for the bill and sighed. 'We seem fated never to finish a conversation. Remind me to talk to you about a party this evening.'

They went out of the café together and started to walk towards the car. 'Shall I run you home first?' he asked.

'My goodness, no—you'll be late, besides if I don't walk I'll get fat.'

He studied her with a leisurely eye and she blushed a little. 'You're very nice as you are,' he assured her, 'especially when you blush.' He got into the car with a casual wave and drove off, and she turned away once he was out of sight and did her shopping and went home. She felt vaguely unhappy, although she had no idea why, and once in the house and immersed in her small chores, she felt better. Indeed, by the time she had fetched Sibella from school and they were downstairs waiting for Benedict to come home she felt that the day was quite perfect. Quite unaccountably her happy mood changed when there was a phone message to say that Benedict wouldn't be able to get home for lunch. He gave no reason, and Prudence, listening to Sibella's chatter as they ate, became more and more preoccupied. Supposing, just supposing he had met Myra—or any of the other women he must have known before he had met herself—he might even now, at this very minute, be lunching somewhere, smiling that slow smile of his at some witticism from his beautiful companion. She frowned so heavily that Sibella interrupted herself to say: 'You look angry— you frown. You are sick, Mama?'

Prudence gave herself a metaphorical shake. 'No, darling, of course not. If you've finished we'll get our things on and take Henry for his walk. It's getting very cloudy, we'd better go quickly before it starts to rain.'

Ork, seeing them out of the house, shook his head at the lowering sky. 'It will rain very much, *mevrouw*,' he observed worriedly. 'Do not go far.'

'Only to the other side of the park, Ork—it makes a good run for Henry, and we can always stand under a tree.'

The wind was sighing and moaning as they crossed the road and ran across the grass to the first avenue, and then, because Henry was already far ahead of them, they walked on to the next avenue, with the busy road well away on one side, and Het Loo Palace on the other. It began to rain as they reached the last stretch of grass and then, with frightening suddenness, the rain turned to hail. Henry, racing round in happy circles, stopped, shook himself and came tearing back towards them. They were all wet by the time they reached the first of the trees, and since the sky was leaden and the hail beat down, Prudence took refuge against one of them, Sibella tucked under one arm, Henry cowering between them.

There was no one else in sight, and although the street lights shone in the distance they seemed a very long way off. 'As soon as it stops we'll run for home,' said Prudence cheerfully. 'We can cut across the grass and be there in no time.'

'We go now?' demanded Sibella. 'I am cold, and so is Henry.'

'We'll all be as warm as toast once we're home, we'll sit by the fire and have our tea.' Prudence's cheerful voice masked doubts as to how soon that would be.

The hail stopped as suddenly as it had begun. Laughing and out of breath, they reached the house and found Ork waiting for them in the hall.

'There is a lady visitor,' he informed Prudence in a disapproving voice. 'She is in the drawing room, *mevrouw.*'

'Oh, lord!' Prudence swept damp hair out of her eyes. 'I'll just go and tidy myself. Would you ask Betje if she would see to Sibella for a minute? I'll be two ticks.'

She flew upstairs behind Sibella, leaving Ork to shake his elderly head and smile as he led Henry away to be dried in the kitchen.

Prudence came downstairs five minutes later, hair still clinging in damp tendrils around her pretty face, sober court shoes in place of the boots she had been

wearing. She was hardly dressed for afternoon calls,
she reflected ruefully—a tweed skirt and a bulky
sweater belted at her slender waist, even though the
belt was a rather splendid Italian one, but there had
been no time to change. She opened the drawing room
door and saw Myra lounging in one of the big chairs,
contemplating her nails.

She didn't get up, only smiled lazily and said:
'Hullo. Do you actually go out walking in this foul
weather? I was driving this way and it seemed a good
idea to call in and offer my felicitations. You stole a
march on all of us, didn't you? Clever you!'

'Did I?' asked Prudence mildly. 'I didn't know.
Thank you for your good wishes. Would you like
coffee—or tea?'

'No, thanks. I'm on my way to the hairdressers. I
always called in when I was driving there—before
your time, of course.' She smiled with quite open
malice. 'Oh, well, all good things come to an end,
don't they? Cosy little lunches and half an hour round
the fire chatting. I suppose Benedict comes home to
lunch now.'

She looked sideways at Prudence. 'Most days, at
any rate—perhaps the cosy little lunches aren't quite
at an end.'

Prudence watched her, her tongue held firmly
between her teeth. Not for the world was she going to
allow Myra to annoy her, only she wished she would
go. She pinned a smile on to her face and after a
silence which went on too long asked: 'You're sure you
won't have coffee?'

Myra uncurled herself from the chair and stood up.
'No thank you Prudence. I had it after lunch.' She
crossed the room, holding out a hand. 'Benedict

always drinks too much of it, you know, you must get him on to your so English tea. Goodbye—I really must fly, I'm late already.'

And as Prudence went with her to the door: 'Don't bother, I know my way around this house rather well, you know.'

She went past Prudence, closing the door quietly behind her and Prudence stood in the middle of the room muttering to herself in what her mother would have called a very ill-bred manner. She stopped for a moment to listen to Myra's voice and tinkling laugh— presumably she was intent on captivating the rather dour Ork.

Only it hadn't been Ork. The door opened again and Benedict came in. He crossed the room to where Prudence was standing, dropped a swift kiss on the top of her head and asked: 'What on earth's Myra doing here?'

'She came to call on her way to the hairdresser.' Prudence's voice was still a little shrill with annoyance. 'We were out—we had to wait under a tree until that hail stopped, and when we got home she was here.'

Benedict turned to look at her, an amused gleam in his eyes. 'Intent on getting up your back, I'll be bound.'

'Well, she didn't,' declared Prudence rather too forcefully. 'I'm sure you can lunch with her every day of the week if you want to!'

He didn't take his eyes off her but the amusement in them changed to something else. He said placidly: 'That's very generous of you, my dear. Now one can see the advantages of a marriage such as ours, based on friendship and respect for each other's right to do as one wishes,' he went on smoothly, 'and see how Sibella is benefiting from a harmonious relationship such as ours.'

Prudence had shot him a quick look; he must be joking, he had sounded so pompous. But he returned her look with a benign one of his own and went on: 'Where is she, by the way?'

'I asked Betje to take her upstairs and change her socks and shoes and dry her up a bit—we all got soaking wet. I didn't know it was Myra, so I just tidied my hair and came straight down again.' She paused. 'Are we really harmonious, Benedict?'

She hadn't meant to say that, it had popped out and she was sorry it had, but suddenly she disliked the idea; it savoured of a milk-and-water existence with Benedict, and it had occurred to her with the speed of light that she had no wish to be a friend. Harmony and respect, as far as she was concerned, could fly out of the window. She contemplated with horror the idea of being tolerant about cosy little lunches and half hours by the fire. Her green eyes flashed at the very idea, and Benedict, watching her still, thought how very beautiful she was when she was put out.

'You make it sound very dull,' he observed, and there was laughter in his voice. 'I can assure you that there is no need for it to be.'

She turned her back on him and looked unseeingly out of the window. He was quite right, of course. To be in harmony with someone, true harmony, must be wonderful, but then of course you'd have to love that person. Like I love you, Benedict, she cried silently, and I've only just this very minute discovered it and now what am I to do?

The problem was solved for her by Sibella's entry,

talking her small head off the moment she entered the room, pouring out the story of their walk to her father, and then begging Prudence in her careful English to have tea just a little earlier. 'For Papa's home, and we always have tea when he is here.'

'An excellent idea, *liefje*. Down here or in the playroom?'

'Here, please, Papa, and may Henry come too? He is hungry.'

So they spent an hour or more having tea and then playing cards, all three of them on the floor with Henry lolling beside them and getting in the way, while Prudence tried not to think about Benedict, so close to her and yet so unreachable. Presently she took Sibella off for her supper and to be put to bed, and then, unwilling to face him until she had got her feelings under control, went along to her room, to change out of the sweater and skirt into a wool dress and do things to her hair and face. Suddenly life was full of problems and she wasn't sure how to cope with them. And she hadn't known that love could be so overwhelmingly powerful; the feeling she had had for Tony had been no more than a schoolgirl's crush.

As she went downstairs she promised herself that she would do her best to make Benedict love her. She had no idea how she was going to set about it, but she would think of something. She crossed the hall and Benedict put his head out of the study door. 'Come in here, will you? There's a letter I want you to read.'

Prudence sat down on the chair he drew up for her, glad that the only light was the powerful desk lamp, so that she was in shadow and could blush in comfort.

'Wait a minute, I'll get us a drink.' Benedict went away and came back with a tray. 'Sherry, Madeira?'

He poured her a glass of sherry and gave himself a whisky, sat down at his desk and handed her the letter.

He was asked to make a short tour of the bigger cities of England; London, of course, Birmingham, Bristol, Liverpool, Oxford, and in Scotland, Edinburgh. It was to last ten days and arrangements would be made for him.

'But that's marvellous,' said Prudence, 'but what's this hypo ... heavens ... hypophosphatasia? Something you know a lot about?'

'I've written a couple of papers on it. It's a deficiency of alkaline phosphates in bone cells. Do you really want to know?'

She nodded, 'Yes.'

He explained. It took some time. Ork came twice to tell them that dinner was waiting, but by then at least Prudence had a very good idea of what Benedict was talking about. And over dinner she went on asking questions, because she was scared that he might start talking about the advantages of a sensible marriage, and she wouldn't be able to bear that.

But she couldn't go on talking for ever, and when she finally petered out with her questions he said abruptly: 'We'll both go—better still, we'll take Sibella with us. Do you suppose Nancy would have her? Or your mother? There'll be quite a lot of travelling for us. Would you like that?'

'I'd love it.' She tried not to sound too excited. 'What about Sibella's school?'

'A few days won't matter. I'll have to fix things up at the hospital and rearrange my appointments, and I've two weeks in which to do it.'

They had gone back to the drawing room to have their coffee when he asked: 'But perhaps you'd rather stay with your parents? Or Nancy? Perhaps that would be a better idea?'

Prudence had no idea how clearly her feelings showed on her face. She said with careful casualness: 'Oh, no—I mean, I can visit them any time, can't I? I should so like to hear you lecture.'

'I'm flattered. We won't say anything to Sibella for a few days or she'll be unmanageable.' He lounged back in his chair, very relaxed. 'Does she need any clothes? We might get them in Arnhem.'

'She needs a new dressing gown and perhaps slippers to match, and if she goes to any parties later on she'll need one or two pretty frocks. Velvet is very fashionable for little girls—she'd look sweet in dark red or sapphire blue.'

He smiled gently. 'Yes—well, get what you think is right for her. And what about our party? Could you cope with one before we go? Informal, I think, so that we can phone invitations. If we have everyone I can think of it'll be over and done with . . .'

'I think you sound as though you don't like parties,' Prudence commented.

'I daresay I'll like them better now you're here to arrange everything.'

They settled on a date and presently Prudence said goodnight and went to bed. She had managed rather well, she considered, sitting there showing just the right amount of interest, not being too eager about going to England with him, stitching away at the embroidery she had brought to work at in the evenings. She'd made rather a hash of it because her hands would shake every time she thought about him, but he wasn't to know that. She would have to unpick it in the morning.

She got ready for bed, mooning round the room, picking things up and putting them down again. If only there were someone she could talk to about it! She remembered the very first time she had met Benedict she had asked his advice; she would have liked to do that now, but that would be impossible. Her mother would be bewildered and quite unable to understand, and Nancy, so happy herself, would only be made unhappy. The prospect of bottling up her love for the rest of her life was daunting. She stared at her reflection in the mirror; her unhappy face stared back at her and presently Prudence, who almost never cried, allowed herself the luxury of a really good weep.

CHAPTER SEVEN

Morning was another day, albeit a nasty damp dark one. Prudence, putting on rather more make-up than usual to hide her pink eyelids, took herself to task. No more crying; it wouldn't help. There was only one thing to do—to go on as she had started, to be as good a wife and companion as possible and to stay Benedict's friend at all costs. That way, who knew, in time, he might love her just a little.

He wasn't at breakfast; he'd been called out during the night and hadn't returned home yet, but halfway through the meal he phoned. He sounded tired. 'I'll be home in about an hour—could you get Sitska to have some breakfast ready for me? I'll shower and shave first. See to the letters, will you? Tell Sibella to be a good girl.'

Prudence went to see Sitska in the kitchen, took Sibella to school and hurried home. There had been no time to look at the post and there were several letters. She had got through them all and arranged them on his desk by the time he got home, and she went into the hall to meet him as he came in.

He was in a sweater and slacks, unshaven and weary, but his 'good morning' was uttered in his usual placid tones.

'Shower first or a cup of tea?' asked Prudence. 'And will fifteen minutes' time do for breakfast?'

'Perfect, and I'll have that tea now.' He took his bag into the study and went across the hall to the sitting room. 'Have one with me?'

'I'll fetch it,' said Prudence and sped away.

'What was it?' she asked when he'd drunk half of his tea. 'Or don't you want to talk about it?'

'Cardiac arrest—that was just after midnight. I was just leaving the hospital when there was a second one on the operating table. It's taken us all this time . . .'

'The patients will be all right?'

'I believe so; it's early days yet, but at least they've got a chance.'

She poured him a second cup. 'Do you have to go back at once? Could you have a quick nap?'

He shook his head. 'Ten minutes at the most. I've a busy morning and I'm running late already.' He smiled, a faint, tired smile that wrenched at her heart. 'I shan't be home to lunch—I shan't be going out either.'

Prudence blushed. 'I'm sorry—I was hateful, wasn't I? I won't do it again. It's none of my business anyway.'

He lifted an eyebrow and gave her a questioning look, but she judged that this was no time to argue. She picked up the tray. 'Ten minutes and Sitska will bring in your breakfast.'

Benedict got up, laughing a little. 'I've been unused to being ordered about like this for years—I rather like it!'

He was back with a minute to spare, shaved and dressed with his usual elegance, only his face was lined and pale. 'When do you have to go again?' asked Prudence, pouring his coffee.

He glanced at the bracket clock on the wall behind her. 'My first appointment is at ten o'clock—at my rooms. I'll have to leave here five minutes before that.'

She nodded and didn't speak while he devoured

toast and cheese and cold ham. When he had drunk his final cup of coffee, she said quietly: 'You've got just over ten minutes. If you lie down, I'll wake you. I told Ork not to come in until I rang, so you won't be disturbed.'

He was asleep at once, stretched out on the wide high-backed sofa along one wall. She sat and looked at him, longing to touch him, not moving until it was time to wake him.

He was alert at once. 'Tea round the playroom fire?' he asked. He didn't wait for an answer, but dropped a kiss on her cheek and went past her into the hall where Ork was waiting. He said something to the old man as he opened the door and Ork smiled widely, then they both turned to look at her before the door was shut and Benedict had gone.

Prudence did the letters then, rearranged the flowers and went along to consult with Sitska about food for the party. They got on rather well by now, and Ork was always at hand to translate. They settled on celery sticks with cream cheese, tiny savoury puffs, vol-au-vents, *bitter balls*, lobster patties and cheese straws. There would be ices and little trifles and gateaux for the sweet-toothed and bowls of hot chestnuts for those who wanted something a bit different. Prudence left the kitchens and went back to the sitting room. She would have her coffee and afterwards deal with the letters. Benedict had left a list of friends to be invited and she had offered to look them up in the phone book and write the numbers beside the names so that they could phone everyone that evening.

She went and got the list now and fetched the phone book, then sat down at the small desk under the window. There were a lot of names, it would take longer than she had thought.

She was halfway through when she heard the clang of the front door bell and Ork's voice in the hall. He appeared a few moments later at the door.

'Professor Herrisma has called, *mevrouw*.'

Prudence flung down her list and jumped to her feet. 'Oh, how nice—ask him to come in, please, Ork. Everard, what a lovely surprise! I was just going to have coffee, do say you'll have it with me. Did you want to see Benedict? He's at the hospital—he was there most of the night too.'

Everard shook the hand she held out and smiled at her, a questioning look in his eyes. 'I didn't expect to see him, but I was passing and I called to see if you would both have dinner with me one evening.'

Prudence sat down and nodded to the other end of the sofa. 'We'd love to,' and she beamed even more widely at him as he sat down beside her. 'We're planning a party quite soon and I don't know when Benedict's free . . .'

'How about Sunday evening, then? I'll ask Mevrouw van der Culp along too.' He fell silent while Ork put the coffee tray on a small table close to Prudence, but when he'd gone again he went on: 'I don't suppose you've got out much since you got back?'

'Hardly at all,' said Prudence cheerfully, 'but we are going to Arnhem on Saturday.' She almost told him about the trip to England, but she wasn't sure if Benedict would like that even though he and Everard were such old friends.

She gave Everard his coffee, happy to have him there because he was Benedict's friend, and perhaps because of that she found herself talking to him as

though she had known him all her life; she told him
about her home and the difficulties she was having
with his language and how Sibella was doing at school,
and because Benedict was uppermost in her mind she
talked a great deal about him too. And Everard
listened stolidly, not saying much, sitting sideways so
that he could watch her. They were discussing dogs
and Henry in particular when the door opened and
Benedict came in. Prudence stopped in mid-sentence
and got to her feet.

'Benedict—heavens, is it so late? I must fetch
Sibella . . .'

He was at his most placid. 'Hullo, my dear.
Everard, how nice to see you. And it's not late,
Prudence—there's still all of half an hour before
Sibella needs to be fetched. I found that I could get
away after all.'

He crossed the room and sat down in his big chair.
'Have I interrupted some interesting discussion?' He
looked at Prudence, smiling faintly, and she frowned a
little. He looked as placid as usual, his voice was just
as slow and quiet, but all the same she had the nasty
feeling that he was angry.

'Dogs,' she explained. 'We were talking about
Henry and Podge. Benedict, you'd like coffee,
wouldn't you? Are you very tired?'

'Ork is bringing me some coffee, and if you mean by
tired that I might wish to have a sleep before lunch, I
don't, thank you.'

The smile he gave her, she decided, wasn't a very
nice one. 'Everard called to see if we'd have dinner
with him.'

'I don't know if you're committed to anything,
Benedict—if you're not how about Sunday evening?'

Benedict watched Prudence pour his coffee. 'That will be delightful. Anyone else going to be there?'

'Mevrouw van der Culp. Prudence tells me that you were at the hospital last night. Anything interesting?'

'A cardiac arrest; I think we've pulled him through—and then a second one in theatre. Dulmin was operating. I thought we'd got him too, but he hasn't made it. That's why I'm home early.'

Everard stood up. 'Well, I'd better be on my way— I've got a list this afternoon . . .'

'Why not stay to lunch?' said Prudence, and wished that she hadn't as she glanced at Benedict's face.

'Yes, why not?' he echoed, But Everard refused in his grave way, shook hands and left the room with Benedict.

It was almost time to fetch Sibella. Prudence picked up the tray and carried it out to the kitchen, to be reprimanded by Ork for doing so, and went back to the sitting room. Benedict was at the desk, looking at the list of guests for their party, and she said guiltily: 'I haven't finished it, but I'll have it ready by teatime.' She added: 'I'm sorry.'

Benedict turned away from the window where he had been staring out at the garden. 'Am I such a hard taskmaster?' he asked mildly.

'Heavens, no, but I said I'd have it ready for you, and it's not.' She added shyly: 'It's nice that you're home early.' She went pink as she said it because she had spoken her thought out loud, something she would have to learn not to do. 'I'll fetch Sibella.'

'And I will go with you.'

She fetched her coat and a scarf for her hair and found him waiting for her. They walked quickly, his arm tucked into hers. She hoped that he couldn't feel her trembling at his touch and because she felt shy and awkward with him, she talked non-stop, mostly about Everard's visit and what they had talked about. And Benedict listened gravely, saying very little, his eyes thoughtful.

Going back home, of course, it was Sibella, dancing along between them, who did all the talking. There was to be a school play at the end of term and she had been chosen to be a fairy. 'You will sew a dress, Mama?' she begged excitedly. 'Juffrouw Smid says it may be any colour...' She lapsed into her own tongue, and Benedict obligingly translated and then suggested that Prudence should go along and see Juffrouw Smid and get the details right.

'Yes, I will,' said Prudence, 'although I'm scared stiff of her. She's very large, you know.'

Benedict laughed. 'Well, don't expect me to go with you. Her English is excellent.'

'I know, better than mine. I must take Dutch lessons, mustn't I?'

'Why, yes. Why not ask Juffrouw Smid to teach you? She could come for an hour or so in the evenings.'

Prudence agreed rather forlornly. That would mean that she wouldn't see so much of him; on the other hand, the sooner she learned to speak his language the more chance she had of making a success of her marriage.

As he opened the door and stood aside to let them pass, she said: 'All right, I will. Will it take long? I mean, to learn Dutch?'

'It's a very difficult language,' he told her as he crossed the hall to his study. 'I'll see you at lunch.'

The conversation was almost entirely in the hands of Sibella during their meal, which was a good thing, for Prudence was discovering that it was difficult to maintain her normal manner with Benedict; of course she would get used to the situation in time, and the quicker the better, and he, who usually carried on an easy flow of general topics, was strangely silent too.

Prudence was conscious of relief when he glanced at his watch and declared that he would have to go. 'The clinic,' he explained, 'but I'll be back in time for tea.' He ruffled Sibella's hair, touched Prudence's shoulder lightly as he passed her chair, and a moment later she heard the car leaving. In three hours' time he would be back again, she thought, and smiled to herself so that Sibella wanted to know if she was happy.

'Yes, darling,' said Prudence, 'and again no.'

'I don't understand, Mama.'

'Nor do I, *liefje*.'

By the time Saturday came she was no nearer getting her thoughts sorted out. She reached the sensible conclusion not to spoil the day by filling her head with foolish longings but to accept what it had to offer and be happy about it. And it was a good day. They drove to Arnhem through the Veluwe, the wooded country on either side of the road all around them, and since it was still fairly early, not much traffic, to spoil the illusion that they were miles away from anywhere. Arnhem, when they reached it, was already busy, though. Benedict parked the car and took them at once to have coffee before escorting them patiently from one shop to the next. There were a number of chic boutiques, and presently he observed mildly: 'Do you know what you're going to buy? There are one or two department stores, but I daresay you prefer to get something in one of these smaller shops.'

'Well—yes.' Prudence was examining a colourful knitted outfit, flung carelessly over a stool in a tiny window. 'I like that . . .'

He said instantly: 'So do I—let's get it.'

It happened to fit her, and although the price was shocking, since Benedict insisted on paying for it—a birthday present, he said vaguely—she felt no guilt squandering so much money. They went back into the street again and this time found a dress and coat for Sibella. 'And shoes,' said Prudence urgently. 'You simply must have another pair for school.'

They found shoes and while they were there, Benedict added a pair of little bronze slippers Sibella had been admiring, and by then it was after noon, and as he pointed out, if they intended to go on shopping after lunch then they might as well go back to the car, get rid of the parcels and go to the hotel.

They lunched at the Savoy, overlooking the river and, from a quick glance at the menu, wildly expensive, thought Prudence. She really would have to get used to having lots of money. Her own family weren't poor by any means, but living on Benedict's scale was rather breathtaking. She did in fact lose her breath entirely when he walked them into a small shop with nothing but a mink hat and a chinchilla stole in its window, and asked to see fur coats. Ranch mink, he told the saleslady firmly, and added to Prudence: 'I don't care for animals being trapped, do you?'

He didn't wait for her to say yes but turned to look at the armful of coats being offered. 'Whichever you like, my dear,' he told her, and Prudence meekly tried them all on, while Sibella danced around begging her to have them all. 'They're pretty, and you are pretty too, Mama,' she declared, and Prudence went a charming pink when her father agreed.

She chose a dark fur finally; it made her hair glow and did wonders for her creamy skin, and when a matching hat was suggested she tried that on too, a small round affair which perched most attractively on top of her head.

Outside on the pavement again, she tried to thank Benedict, but he brushed her thanks aside very gently. 'Delighted to give you a belated wedding present, Prudence,' he told her placidly. 'Let's go and look at books.'

Holland, Prudence had discovered from her limited experience, had some splendid bookshops. The three of them spent half an hour and came out loaded.

'It's too late for the open air museum today,' said Benedict, 'but we'll go next time we come this way. Let's have tea now.'

A lovely day, thought Prudence drowsily as she lay half asleep that night. Benedict had been such fun, the kind of companion one so often dreamed of and never found. She had felt smug in his company, seeing the glances other women gave him. He wasn't just a handsome man, he was elegant too, and self-assured, the kind of man one could leave to see to everything. She closed her eyes and dreamed of him; not quite satisfactorily, for she awoke before the end and was left with a vague elusive feeling. Dreams never turned out as you wanted them to.

But they didn't matter once she was up and breakfasting, with Sibella chattering non-stop and Benedict rumbling goodnatured answers from time to time. They went to church later and after lunch took Henry for a walk. Prudence's day was perfect. She

would have preferred to have spent the evening at
home with Benedict, but after all, Everard was a close
friend and she liked Mevrouw van der Culp.

She put Sibella to bed, made sure that her own
hair and face were at their best, then went
downstairs to where Benedict was waiting. The drive
was a short one, and she regretted that, for there
was no time to do more than pass a few desultory
remarks before they drew up before Everard's house.
It was not to be compared with Benedict's home—
red brick and far too many fussy bits of plaster work
above the windows. The front door was painted dark
green, and they went up steps to reach it before
Benedict tugged at an old-fashioned bell pull beside
it. The elderly woman who answered the door suited
the house very well. She had a severe no-nonsense
face, and iron-grey hair rigidly waved, moreover she
was severely dressed in black. But her face melted
into a broad smile when she saw Benedict and she
said something delightedly which made him laugh.
'Prudence, this is Nessie, Everard's housekeeper.
We're very old friends.'

Prudence shook hands and murmured, '*Aangenaam*',
and Nessie broke into further speech which he
patiently translated. 'She's congratulating us on our
marriage and wishing us all the best.'

Prudence smiled at them both and then turned, her
smile widening, as Everard came into the hall.
'Everard—hullo,' she glanced round her at the rather
overpowering size of the square hall. 'What an
enormous house you've got!'

'Too big for an old bachelor like myself.' He took
her hand and smiled, then turned to Benedict. 'Glad
you could come—you're not on call?'

Benedict shook her head. 'After midnight. Is Godmother here?'

'In the drawing-room.' He waited while Nessie took Prudence's coat, then led the way to a half open door and ushered them inside.

The room was vast, high-ceilinged and furnished with old-fashioned heavily upholstered chairs and a number of awkward little tables—the kind of room a bachelor could live in for years and not notice just how awful it was. Everard needed a wife. Prudence crossed the room with her host and greeted Mevrouw van der Culp, who gave her a cheek to kiss, asked how she was, then turned to kiss Benedict. When they were all sitting sipping pre-prandial drinks, the old lady asked: 'And when is the party to be? I look forward to it.'

'We've just finished making out a list of guests, but since you're both here and such old friends, it's on Tuesday week. There'll be about thirty, I should think . . .'

'Quite time too,' observed Mevrouw van der Culp. 'It's high time you entertained again, Benedict.' She added: 'Of course, you were younger then.'

He didn't reply, and Prudence was aware that he was for once at a loss for an answer. Perhaps when he had been married before, he and his first wife had led a social life; she felt a sharp stab of jealousy at the thought.

The evening was spent pleasantly enough. Dinner was eaten in a sombre room, heavy with dark oak and a great chandelier which somehow didn't light the room adequately, but if the light was dim, the conversation wasn't. Mevrouw van der Culp was a witty old lady with a clever tongue, and both Everard and Benedict played up to her.

They went back to the drawing-room for coffee and presently Everard offered to show Prudence the house. As they crossed the hall he told her: 'I keep meaning to alter the furnishings and the curtains and so on, but it doesn't seem worth the trouble, living as I do, by myself. If I were to marry it would be a different matter, of course.'

Prudence stopped in the middle of a small, sombre sitting room. 'Haven't you ever wanted to marry?' she asked.

'Yes, twice, once when I was very young, just qualified and full of dreams, and the second time . . . when I met you, Prudence.'

She went a little pale, then red. 'Oh, my goodness, Everard, you can't mean that!'

'But I do. Don't worry, it won't make any difference to our being friends. Besides, Benedict and I have known each other for most of our lives. I would never do anything to hurt him—or you.' He smiled slowly. 'You know, I thought, just for a little while, that I might have had a chance with you, but of course I soon saw that I hadn't. You have no idea how happy I am to see the pair of you married, you're so right for each other.'

She put out a hand and touched his sleeve. 'Everard, I'm so sorry, I really am. You'll stay my friend as well as Benedict's, won't you? What happened to the other girl?'

He shrugged his shoulders. 'She married and went abroad to live. I have no idea where she is now.'

'What was her name?'

'Joanne—Joanne Winkeler. She had red hair too.'

'And you are still in love with her, aren't you? I look like her . . .'

She reached up and kissed his cheek, and he caught her hands in his. 'Yes, green eyes and glorious hair.' He smiled a little. 'She had a temper to match!'

'So have I, Everard. I do things on the spur of the moment.'

'Like marrying Benedict?'

'Yes.' She turned her head at a faint sound from the doorway. Benedict was there, but whether he'd been standing there for any length of time she had no means of knowing. She thought not, for he said in his calm way: 'There you are. Everard, this room is truly hideous, you really must get it changed. Prudence, Godmother wants to go home, we'll give her a lift. It will save Everard getting out his car.' He wandered into the room. 'Have you told Everard that we are going to England in a few weeks?'

Prudence blinked; something in his voice didn't sound like him at all. 'No, I didn't—I didn't think of it, and even if I had I wouldn't have,' she added with a fine disregard for grammar. 'Everard, thank you for a lovely evening, we'll see you at the party perhaps before then—at least, I expect you two see each other most days at the hospital.'

She went to find Mevrouw van der Culp and presently they left, the old lady stowed carefully on the back seat. If she had been tired she showed no sign of it now, and indeed, when they reached her house and saw her indoors she assured Prudence that she never went to bed before midnight.

'I love going out in the evenings,' she went on. 'And I'm always the last to go.' She laughed at herself, kissed a puzzled Prudence and went indoors with a laughing remark to Benedict, as he kissed her goodnight.

'Well, Mevrouw van der Culp recovered quickly,'
observed Prudence as they drove back home. 'Was she
tired or did she just want to go home?'

'She wasn't in the least tired,' said Benedict coolly.
'It was I who wanted to leave and she gave me the
excuse.'

'Oh, I see.' She didn't see at all, but she wasn't
going to say so.

'I expect you've got some work to do, and you're on
call after midnight, too.'

If she had hoped that he would agree with her she
was to be disappointed. He grunted something she
didn't catch and she started on the safer topic of their
evening. 'That's a very old-fashioned house,' she
remarked, 'but it could be made quite a show place.
Everard ought to get himself a wife.' But Benedict
didn't answer that either, so she gave up. It didn't
matter really, being silent; he was close to her and she
loved him so much that even sitting beside him was a
joy.

It wasn't late by the time they got in. Prudence went
upstairs to make sure that Sibella was sleeping and
then went to the drawing room.

'I asked Ork if we could have coffee. You'd like a
cup?'

Benedict was standing by the fire, reading a note
which had come by hand for him. He looked up
without smiling. 'Why not? I'll be out tomorrow. I'll
have to leave early, so explain to Sibella, will you?'

She said steadily: 'Yes, of course. Will you be back
before she goes to bed?'

'I doubt it.' He went and sat down and she poured
their coffee. 'Everard suggested that you drove over to
the Kroller-Muller Museum. Why don't you give him

a ring and suggest tomorrow afternoon? Sibella's a bit young for it, but she would enjoy the drive.'

Prudence said without hesitation: 'Oh, no, I don't think so—it would bore her to tears. I'll take my car and we'll drive somewhere and have tea out. She likes that.'

'You don't like Everard?' The question was casual, and she, her thoughts busy as to why he had to spend the whole day away from home without choosing to tell her why, answered just as casually. 'Oh, yes, very much—he's one of the nicest men I've ever met.' She smiled across at him. 'Isn't that a good thing? Just suppose I'd disliked him on sight, or him me—how awkward it would have been for you!'

He glanced up from his letter again without speaking, his eyes cold, so that she asked quite sharply: 'Is something the matter, Benedict—there's something wrong?'

She must be imagining things. His 'Of course not' was uttered with smiling calm.

Sibella was inclined to be upset when Prudence told her at breakfast that they would be spending the day on their own, but she cheered up when Prudence suggested that they should let her choose what they should do. 'Church first, of course, but we'll have lunch somewhere if you like, think about it quickly so that I can let Sitska know.'

'The Zoo,' said Sibella after scarcely a moment's thought. 'In Rhenen, I went once with Papa, and we ate there too.'

'Fine, that's where we'll go, then. But we'll come home for tea, just in case Papa gets back early.'

They got out a map when they got back from church, and Prudence was relieved to find that

Rhenen wasn't far—twenty miles or so, and easy
enough to get to. They drove off under the fatherly
eye of Ork, into a morning which was going, unless
she was much mistaken, to turn into a wet afternoon.

She took a quieter road across the centre of the
Veluwe, avoiding the towns until she came to Ede and
then taking an even smaller road to Wageningen and
then on to Rhenen. The Zoo was on the near side of
the little town, and she found it easy enough to park
the car, buy their tickets and take Sibella straight to
the restaurant, pleasantly old-fashioned in an ancient
watch-tower, and she was kept busy answering
Sibella's questions and eating lunch, which prevented
her thinking too much about Benedict. And later,
walking about the Zoo and the park, with the little girl
demanding the names in English of all the animals, she
banished him from her mind and joined in the child's
pleasure. They were driving home again when she
started to worry once more, although she told herself
unendingly that she had no reason to do so, but when
Sibella put a small paw on her knee and asked her
anxiously why she was sad, she conjured up a very
credible laugh. 'Not a bit of it, darling—was I
frowning? I often do when I'm driving. We've had a
lovely afternoon, haven't we? Such a pity Papa
couldn't come too.' I wonder where he is? she added
silently, and had her answer within seconds. The
Aston Martin with Benedict at the wheel and Myra
beside him slid past on the main road they were
waiting to turn into, and going away from Appeldoorn,
too. Sibella hadn't seen it. Prudence, feeling sick,
joined the traffic to Appeldoorn, wishing with all her
heart that she could have turned the car in the
opposite direction and followed Benedict. A rush of

fury shook her. No wonder he hadn't said where he was going! Just let him wait till he got back home; there were a few questions he could answer . . .

'Mama,' shrilled Sibella, 'you've gone past our road!'

With an effort Prudence pulled herself together, turned the car in the teeth of several indignant drivers and drove carefully to their own doorstep. Ork opened the door before she could get her key out and Henry came tearing from the kitchen to jump all over them. It was easier to think straight in familiar surroundings; Prudence took Sibella upstairs to take off her outdoor things and then went with her to the drawing-room. She had suggested that they should have their tea in the playroom, but the little girl shook her head. 'Always we have tea in the drawing-room on Sundays, and Papa will come.'

Only he didn't. Prudence, filling in the gap between tea and Sibella's supper, played cards, Ludo and Snakes and Ladders, countering her anxious enquiries as to where Papa was by what she hoped were sensible answers. He still was absent as Prudence helped Sibella to bed, and although she stayed for a while, reading to the child, there was no sign of him.

'I tell you what,' said Prudence, 'when Papa comes in, I'll ask him to come here and kiss you goodnight, even if you're asleep. How will that do?'

A rather tearful Sibella agreed, and presently she fell asleep and Prudence was free to go downstairs again.

She had her dinner on a tray, eating it hastily and carrying the barely touched contents back to the kitchen, and at Sitska's surprised concern, inventing a headache. 'I'll have a bath and get ready for bed,' she told Ork, 'and then come down and read until the doctor gets back. Don't wait up; if Sitska will leave coffee ready and the rest of the soup, I can make sandwiches if he needs them.'

Ork demurred, but she was firm. 'We'll lock up—you always go round the windows and doors anyway, don't you? If you do that it will only be the front door.'

She took her time getting ready for bed and then, wrapped in the new blue quilted dressing gown she had bought only that week, padded downstairs to sit by the drawing room fire. Ork appeared almost at once with the coffee tray, fidgeted around the room for a minute or two and then asked:

'*Mevrouw* will be all right? The doctor would not wish that you are alone.'

Prudence was touched at the old man's concern. 'I'll be fine, Ork, and I promise I'll call you if I need to.'

'You will not answer the door, *mevrouw*?'

'No, I promise you, Ork.'

They wished each other goodnight and she heard him going methodically from room to room, making everything secure for the night. Presently the house was quiet save for the tick-tocking of the great Friese clock in the hall and the hurried tripping of the carriage clock on the mantelpiece above her. Now and then the house eased itself gently with gentle creaks and faint whispers, but presently they were drowned by the wind sighing through the trees near the house—all sounds that Prudence found soothing. One of the novels she had bought in Arnhem was on her lap, so was a Dutch dictionary, but presently she closed them both and then her eyes.

The clock was striking one when she woke to the

sound of Benedict's key in the door. She heard him pause in the hall, fling his coat down and then cross the hall. As he came through the door she sat upright.

'I want a word with you,' she began, instant temper taking over from sleep.

'Now?' asked Benedict mildly. 'Do you know the time?'

'You ask me that?' She was so indignant that she stuttered. 'And if you want coffee or something to eat you'll have to get it for yourself. I sent Ork to bed hours ago.'

'So that you could lie in wait for me?' he asked silkily.

'Yes. I saw you this afternoon—with Myra . . .'

'I know. I half expected you to come racing after me.'

'It never entered my head,' she lied. 'If you were going to spend the day—and half the night—with her, why couldn't you have said so?'

He raised his eyebrows. 'My dear Prudence, I don't think that would have been a very wise thing to do. You might have got all sorts of ideas into that fiery head of yours.'

He had gone to sit down opposite to her, most annoyingly calm. 'That's a pretty blue gown. It suits you.'

Prudence all but ground her teeth. 'Never mind that!' she snapped. 'It was a mercy Sibella didn't see you!'

'I'm sure you would have found some very good reason for my—er—lapse.' Benedict smiled at her gently. 'I had no idea you would be on that road.'

She bounced with rage. 'You're insufferable! I wish I'd gone with Everard, and then I wouldn't have seen you!'

His voice was as gentle as his smile. 'I did suggest it.' He got up. 'I'm going to get some coffee. Do you want any? And aren't you going to ask me why I spent the day—these were your words, Prudence—with Myra?'

'I have no wish to know.' Her voice came out rather squeakily for she was on the edge of tears. 'And I don't want any coffee.' She jumped up out of her chair and sailed from the room without looking at him or saying goodnight. It was a great relief to get into bed and cry her eyes out, although she didn't bother to ask herself just why she was weeping. She only knew that she was unhappier than she had ever been in her life.

CHAPTER EIGHT

MORNING brought common sense with it. She should have held her tongue and said nothing to Benedict; they were friends, they had married with a very clear idea of what they were doing and friends trusted each other; she had demonstrated very clearly that she didn't trust him—worse, that she was jealous. She had been a fool, and the only thing to do was to pretend that it had never happened. She went down to breakfast hand in hand with Sibella, greeted Benedict cheerfully, and entered into an unnecessarily long and involved account of their afternoon's outing. She ground to a halt presently, aware that he was silently laughing at her, although he appeared to be giving her his full attention. She crumbled some toast and asked him briskly if he would be in for lunch, not quite looking him in the eye, and when he said that he would, ask about the invitations for the party. 'I've got the ones from the hospital on your desk,' she told him, still brisk despite the twinkle in his eyes, 'but I don't know what to do with the rest.'

'I'll see to them, though you could phone the Brands and the Pennicks—and don't forget Juffrouw Smit. Godmother too, and of course Everard.'

He left the house soon after, dropping a casual kiss on her cheek as he passed by her chair. So everything was to be just as before; the unpleasant little episode was to be forgotten. Next time, and she felt sure that there would be a next time, she would have to seethe and boil behind a friendly, unnoticing face. She gave an indignant snort at the very idea and Sibella asked her if she had a cold.

There wasn't anything much for her to do on a Monday morning, as most of the shops were shut anyway. She took Henry for his walk, phoned her invitations and then decided to go into the town and post some letters, and since it was a grey windy day, she stopped for coffee at one of the fashionable little cafés in the main street. She had bought a Dutch paper, and now over her coffee she began to pick out the headlines. It was more interesting than looking up words in a dictionary. She was beginning to say a few words now, thanks to Benedict and Sibella's help, but the written word was another matter. She was wrestling with the small ads when she heard a voice give a name she had never expected to hear. It was a woman's voice, and Prudence turned round cautiously and took a look. A woman in her late thirties, pretty still and with hair as red as Prudence's own. She glanced up, and Prudence wasn't in the least surprised to see that her eyes were vividly green. Everard's first love, here, only a mile or so from him! The woman smiled faintly, turned to her companion and said something and got up to go. As she went past Prudence's table, Prudence put out an urgent hand.

'Please, could I speak to you? You are Joanne Winkler, aren't you? I heard you . . .'

The woman had stopped. 'Have we met somewhere?' she asked pleasantly. 'You're English—perhaps in the States?'

'We've not met. Everard Herrisma told me about you.'

The woman went white, said something to her

companion, who walked on, then sat down opposite Prudence.

'He is well? Still working at the hospital, perhaps? I only arrived yesterday, I was going to enquire . . .'

'But not going to see him?' asked Prudence.

'No. I—we parted many years ago, he will have forgotten me.'

'He hasn't. He's as in love with you now as he always was.' Prudence made the sweeping statement without hesitation. 'It's a miracle, you know, finding you here, right under his nose.' She hesitated. 'Forgive me for being nosey, but are you married?'

'A widow. I came back . . .' Joanne shrugged her shoulders. 'I smashed my dream all that time ago, I don't expect to pick up the pieces.'

'But you'd like to see Everard?'

Her companion's face puckered. 'Oh, yes, so very much! You see, I made a mistake, and married the wrong man, but I was too proud to do anything about it. And he never wrote.'

'No—well, he wouldn't. Look, I'm not meaning to interfere, but will you let me tell Everard that you're here—get him used to the idea before you meet?' Prudence added, a little pink: 'I'm married to Benedict van Vinke. Did you know him?'

'Of course I did. Everard's good friend and mine also.' A guarded look came over her face. 'He was married . . .' she began uncertainly.

'Yes, but his wife died. He had a little girl, Sibella.'

Joanne said slowly: 'They weren't happy, you know. She was a feather-headed creature. One shouldn't speak ill of the dead, should one, but it's true, and Benedict was a fine doctor even then. They'd only been married—oh, less than a year, when I left, and I

could see . . .' She smiled. 'I'm sure you are a very
good wife for him.'

'I try to be. Look, I've just had an idea. We're
having a small party next week, just drinks and talk for
an hour or two. Will you come? And I won't tell
Everard you're here . . . but perhaps I'd better,
someone is sure to do that. Anyway, you could see him
there, it might be easier with a lot of people around.'

'Yes? You think so? Perhaps you are right.' Joanne
laughed. 'We should agree, should we not, with our
red hair and green eyes? I will do as you say. What a
strange conversation we are having—I don't even
know your name!'

'Prudence. It's a silly name for someone with red
hair, isn't it?'

Joanne laughed. 'I'm glad you weren't prudent. You
might not have talked to me. Is Benedict still living in
his nice house near Het Loo?'

'Yes. I'll see Everard as soon as possible and tell
him. I'm sure everything's going to be all right. I must
go, I have to fetch Sibella from school.' Prudence paid
her bill and they left the café together and parted on
the pavement, and Prudence, walking briskly into the
teeth of the wind, reflected that life could be very
unexpected. With hindsight she realised that she had
been a bit impetuous, buttonholing Joanne like that;
she could have been horribly snubbed. 'Fools walk in,'
she reminded herself, and waved gaily to Sibella,
coming out of school.

The sight of Benedict sitting opposite her at lunch
diverted her thoughts, but when he had gone again
and she and Sibella and Henry were having their walk,
she resolutely put him behind her and concentrated on
her plans to get Everard and Joanne together again,

and the moment they were back home and Sibella had gone off to the kitchen to help get the tea tray ready, she went to the telephone. Everard wasn't home; she had half expected that, so she rang the hospital and gave a sigh of relief when a voice told her that he was there.

Everard was talking to Benedict in the consultants' room when his bleep stopped him in mid-sentence. He went to the phone in a corner of the room and Benedict said: 'I'll see you on the ward, then,' and went out of the room, only to turn round and come in again because he had forgotten the notes he had been discussing. He was through the open door and his hands were on the notes when he heard Everard say: 'Prudence, you mean that? Where are we to meet? At your house? I can hardly wait! Don't tell anyone yet.'

He had his back to Benedict, who stood for a moment looking at his friend before he turned on his heel and left the room again. He had a round to do and did it, looking and talking in his usual calm manner. Only the elderly Ward Sister in Men's Medical, who had known him for years, wondered what was the matter with him, and knowing him so well, didn't ask.

True to her word, Prudence said nothing to Benedict, although she longed to do so. Instead she talked about food and drink for the guests, the new dress she planned for Sibella, and kept him posted as to those who were coming. Everyone they had invited, in fact. Prudence, allowing Sibella to choose between a rich dark blue and a mulberry red velvet dress, pondered her own dress. Something suitable, she decided. Benedict was well known and well liked and had a large circle of friends, even if not all of them would be at their party. Something dignified, she thought, pearl grey or black—she never wore black, but if Benedict thought it would be the right thing she would do so. To her surprise, when she suggested it, he reacted quite violently. 'Good God, no—I loathe women in little black dresses. Pale mauve, if you like, or a nice chocolate brown.'

So she searched the shops for either the one or the other, and came home with a lilac crêpe with a demure neckline and a cleverly cut skirt. She bought kid slippers to match and tried them for Sibella's benefit, with the strict instruction that on no account was her papa to know anything about it.

On the evening of the party, she dressed Sibella and then herself, and they went downstairs together, red velvet and lilac blending very nicely. They went hand in hand into the drawing room where Benedict was sitting reading by the fire. He got up when they went in and stood studying them both. 'Delightful,' he delared. 'You both look as pretty as pictures. My compliments, Prudence.'

'Sibella chose her own dress,' volunteered Prudence. 'It's pretty, isn't it?'

He nodded. 'I'm proud of my daughter.' He didn't say that he was proud of his wife, although Prudence hoped that he would.

'Remember, *liefje*, you go to bed the moment Mama tells you to.' He smiled across at Prudence. 'Everything looks very nice indeed,' he told her. 'You must have worked hard.'

'No,' not really. Ork and Sitska and Betje did most of it. I'm glad you're pleased.' She smiled back at him, so disturbed because he was somehow very remote. If Sibella hadn't been there she would have asked him if there was anything the matter. And anyway, there was no time. The front door bell clanged and she could hear Ork bidding the first of their guests welcome.

It was surprising the number of friends Benedict had. She went among them with him and Sibella dancing along beside her and they were all smiling and friendly, and since they knew each other, in no time at all everyone was talking at the top of his or her voice. The party was a success.

'This is the first social occasion Benedict has hosted for I don't know how long,' a tall stout woman with a loud voice told Prudence. 'His first wife didn't like any of us, you know, we bored her stiff, so he gradually stopped asking us round, and when she died he cut himself off from everyone.' She laughed loudly and quite without malice. 'Of course he's been no monk, but you'd hardly expect that, would you? We are all so delighted that he has married again, my dear, and to such a sensible girl too.'

Prudence answered politely, and presently excused herself as Ork came towards her. He murmured in her ear and her face lit up so that Benedict watching her from the other side of the room, frowned a little. He saw her slip from the room and presently return with Everard, whom she left with a group of friends before rejoining the people she had been talking too. She hadn't looked in his direction once. Ten minutes later Ork appeared again, and once more she slipped from the room, and this time it was five minutes before she returned. When she came back she had Joanne Winkeler with her. Several of the guests recognised her at once and crowded round to greet her before Benedict could reach her. They stood back a little as he took her hand and kissed her cheek. 'My dear Joanne, what a delightful surprise! We all thought you were in the States. You know everyone here, don't you?' He shot a lightning glance at Prudence. 'Including Prudence,' he added blandly. 'You've already met, I take it? Come and meet everyone . . .'

People began to talk again and Prudence walked around with Sibella's hand tucked in hers, saying a bit here and there, all the while wondering how Everard and Joanne would behave when they were actually face to face. She felt cheated, she would have liked to have been there to see, but Benedict had Joanne by the arm still and was steering her gently towards Everard, talking to two elderly ladies. Benedict detached these from his friend with practised ease and left him and Joanne together, pausing to murmur in Everard's ear as he went. Out of the corner of her eye Prudence saw them go through the half open door to the conservatory beyond; so far, so good.

The party was getting into its stride now. Benedict was a good host. Groups formed and reformed, all talking at the tops of their voices, while Ork circulated with drinks and Betje handed the food. It was, Prudence discovered reluctantly, time for Sibella to go to bed. She sent the child to say goodnight to her father and then make a round of the guests, shaking hands politely with each one. 'I haven't said goodnight to Oom Everard or that pretty lady!' shrilled Sibella, as Prudence urged her to the door.

'They are very old friends, darling, and they haven't seen each other for a long time. I'll say goodnight and goodbye to them both for you.'

Sibella was still a little excited. The new dress had to be admired before it was taken off, and the delights of the evening discussed, so it was almost half an hour before Prudence went downstairs again. It was

Mevrouw van der Culp who asked her: 'Where have you been, my dear? Several of us missed you.'

'I'm sorry—Sibella is too small to put herself to bed and she was a little excited.' Prudence glanced casually round the room and paled a little. Myra was there, talking to Benedict and Dr Brand. As usual, thought Prudence sourly, she looked stunning; her scarlet dress outshone every other woman's in the room. Prudence instantly felt dowdy. She left Mevrouw van der Culp with Mevrouw Brand and made her way across the room.

'How nice to see you, Myra, I'm so glad you could come.' In her own ears her voice sounded falsely bright, but it took Myra by surprise.

She said a little uncertainly: 'Oh, hullo, I thought I'd surprise you.' She put a hand on Benedict's coat sleeve and glanced up at him through false eyelashes.

'I like surprising people,' she murmured, and smiled up at him.

Benedict glanced at her with only polite interest. 'Yes. You must excuse me, I must have a word with Juffrouw Smit. Prudence, come with me, will you? It's about your lessons.'

They paused to talk as they went and when they reached Juffrouw Smit, that formidable lady kept them for several minutes. She confessed herself intrigued at the idea of teaching Prudence Dutch and took her time arranging suitable times for her lessons. 'You'll learn quickly enough,' she decided presently. 'You're an intelligent young woman and I believe you really want to learn.'

'Oh, I do,' Prudence assured her. 'I promise you I'll work hard if you will teach me.' Someone joined them and presently she circulated again. It was an hour or more later, when the guests were beginning to go, when she saw Everard and Joanne, and even from the other end of the big room she could see that they looked mightily pleased with themselves. But she couldn't join them for the moment. She stood beside Benedict, shaking hands and being kissed and then thanked, making promises to go to lunch, tea, coffee, and dinner when Benedict had a free evening. She didn't remember half of them, she was too conscious of Benedict close by her.

Mevrouw van der Culp was among the last to go. She offered a cheek to Benedict, then pecked at Prudence. 'A lovely party, my dear—what a blessing you are to Benedict! I see that Joanne and Everard are together again. I wonder who arranged that they should meet here?' She beamed at Prudence. 'You clever girl!'

Hard on her heels came Everard and Joanne. They kissed Prudence and Everard said: 'I can never thank you enough, my dear. We are going to get to know each other again. It's like a miracle, that you should have heard Joanne in that café, Prudence, and done something about it.'

'And kept it a secret,' interposed Benedict dryly.

'That was because I said I wished it,' said Joanne quickly, 'so you do not blame Prudence, please.' She put on the coat that Everard was holding for her. 'And now I shall go with Everard and we shall talk.' She kissed Prudence. 'I will ring you tomorrow, Prudence.'

They drove away together and Prudence turned away from the door as Benedict closed it. She said carefully: 'I'm sorry I didn't tell you about Everard and Joanne. She made me promise—she was afraid that Everard wouldn't want anything to do with her, you see, so I said I'd tell him.'

She stopped as Benedict laughed. 'What's funny?' she asked.

'You phoned him at the hospital, didn't you?' And when she nodded. 'I overheard, quite by accident, and I thought you and he . . .'

Her eyes flashed greenly. 'You did? You thought we were making a date—or something?'

He was leaning against a wall table, his hands in his pockets. 'The thought did cross my mind.' He sounded amused.

She stuttered with rage. 'But I'm married to you— we've only been married for a few weeks . . . how could you even think such a thing?'

He said silkily: 'Quite easily, my dear, in my present state of mind.'

Prudence was without words and so indignant that she hardly heard him. 'And another thing,' she went on, her voice shrill. 'Why did you ask Myra to come? You never said you were going to.'

Benedict was still lounging against the table watching her. 'I didn't invite her; I supposed you did. I spent a good part of the evening wondering why.' And as she opened her mouth once more: 'No, don't say anything else, my dear, I daresay you are tired. It was a very successful evening, thanks to your efforts. What time are we dining?'

'Sitska will have a meal ready at nine o'clock.'

'Splendid. Come and have a drink first.'

'I do not want a drink,' said Prudence distinctly, 'and I do not want dinner either. I'm going to bed.' She began to climb the wide staircase.

For such a large man Benedict could move very fast;

she was no further than the third tread when he was there beside her. 'You're angry with me,' he said gently. 'You believe I don't trust you. I'm sorry, but if you think about it there is another side to it, you know.'

'Oh, pooh!' Her red hair had got the better of her good sense, she galloped upstairs and into her room, where she flung herself on the bed and burst into tears.

So much for their sensible marriage based on friendship and trust and all the rest of that nonsense, and so much for falling in love with him too! A lot of good that had done her; he'd actually thought that she was encouraging Everard! 'And serve him right if I had,' she mumbled into the pillows, 'and if that's all he thinks of me then I'd better go away and he can go back to being a bachelor again, and I hope,' she added waspishly, 'that Myra gets her claws into him!'

Her face was sodden with tears by now, her eyes puffed up and her nose pink, and presently she fell into an exhausted sleep. She woke in the early hours of the morning, very cold, and undressed and got into bed and started to cry all over again.

She looked terrible in the morning, and explained away her puffy eyes and white cheeks to Sibella with the excuse that she had a cold—a piece of news which Sibella lost no time in conveying to her father when they reached the breakfast table. 'You must give her medicine, Papa,' cried the little girl. 'Mama must be well enough to come to England with us, mustn't she?'

Prudence put down her coffee cup. 'Are we all going?' she asked, her gaze focused a few inches above Benedict's head.

'Naturally.' He was studying her face with interest.

'I phoned your mother last night, as well as Nancy. They would both like to have Sibella to stay while we are travelling.'

Prudence took a piece of toast and broke it into a good many small pieces; it gave her something to do. 'Perhaps I could . . .' She got no further.

'No, Prudence, you will be going with me.' His placid voice held a steely note she had seldom heard.

Oh, well, she told herself silently, that's his lookout. I shan't talk he'll be so fed up with me by the time the tour is over. The unbidden thought that she would be with him for a whole ten days crossed her mind. At any other time she would have been in the seventh heaven. She could, of course, fall ill . . . She frowned at her toast, deciding on something suitable; toothache, perhaps migraine, only she'd never had one. A tummy bug? He would pounce on them all and banish them with an antibiotic. She sighed not quite silently, and Benedict observed mildly: 'It would never do to alter our plans now, would it, Prudence? I wouldn't like Sibella to be disappointed.'

She buttered a fragment of toast and put it back on her plate. It was so unfair, he always got the better of her, and that without raising his voice in the very least.

Joanne telephoned during the morning. She was bubbling over with happiness. 'It is just as though we'd never been apart,' she explained. 'Everard feels just the same as I do. I just can't believe it, Prudence, and we can't thank you enough. And since all our friends saw us last night we shan't have the awful business of explaining to them.' She giggled. 'Falling in love is such fun, isn't it?'

When Prudence agreed with suitable enthusiasm she

said: 'You'll both have to come to dinner one evening soon; we've such a lot to talk about.'

Several people phoned to thank her for the party and enough flowers came to keep her busy arranging them for the rest of the day. They all bore little thank-you cards, and she read them all carefully and set them on one side so that she could phone their senders later. It was almost time to fetch Sibella when the last flowers were delivered—red roses, and the accompanying card was in Benedict's handwriting. 'Thank you for making the evening such a success. Benedict.'

Prudence looked at them for a long moment, then she crossed the hall to the garden room where the rest of the flowers were waiting to be arranged. There was a bin in one corner; she stuffed the roses into it and smashed down the lid, then went to get ready to fetch Sibella.

Benedict was already home when they got back. He came out of his study as they went in, remarking that he had taken three phone calls since he'd been in the house and a bunch of flowers from Mevrouw Brand. 'I've put them with the others in the garden room,' he told her. 'Did you get my roses?'

She had felt dreadful ever since she had thrown them into the bin. Now she went quite white while she tried to think what to say. Not that there was any choice. As Sibella danced off to take off her outdoor things, she crossed the hall. 'Yes, I did. They're here.'

She led the way back to the garden room and took the lid off the bin. 'I don't know why I did it,' she whispered. 'At least, I do in a muddled kind of way, but I can't explain.'

His voice was harsh. 'You have no need to do that. It was foolish of me to send them.'

She peeped up at him and was shaken to see his face—sad, resigned, not angry in the least. Which made it so much worse.

She turned away and went upstairs and tidied herself for lunch, and when she eventually went downstairs again he and Sibella were on the floor in the sitting room, with Henry between them, looking at a book together.

He looked up as she went in and his manner was so exactly the same as usual that she wondered for a moment if she had dreamed those awful few minutes. 'Come and see this,' he invited her. 'It's a copy of *The Wind in the Willows*—in English. I thought we might read it to Sibella. I loved it when I was small, didn't you?'

She said yes, not looking at him. She felt guilty and incredibly mean and so ashamed of herself, even though she reminded herself that he was to blame because he hadn't trusted her, but two blacks don't make a white, as her father used to say. She went and sat down beside Sibella and admired Mr Toad in the delightful illustrations.

There was no way of knowing how Benedict felt. His manner towards her during lunch was just as it always was, and yet for a moment, when she had told him about the flowers, he had looked so terrible that she had wanted to put her arms round him and tell him that she loved him. That would have been silly, of course; he wouldn't have believed her, with the roses lying in ruins between them, and even if he had, it would have put him in a frightful spot. It was a relief when he told her after lunch that he would be going to Utrecht that afternoon and would probably not be home until late in the evening. 'Don't keep dinner—

I'll have something at the hospital. Can you cope with the letters? They're from friends in London who want to see us if we have the time.'

'What do you want me to say?' she asked.

'We'll ring them when we're there and arrange something. Oh, and Myra telephoned this morning and left a message. She's leaving for Italy to spend the winter there; she was almost anxious that I shouldn't forget to tell you.'

'Oh, I wonder why?'

Benedict's eyes gleamed with amusement. 'And I was to tell you that she knew when she was beaten.'

'I can't think what she meant,' said Prudence with a heightened colour. She plunged into a series of futile remarks about nothing at all, and he in his blandest manner most obligingly egged her on.

She filled her empty evening planning their trip to England. Now that Sibella was to go with them there were her clothes to see to as well as her own; it kept her nicely occupied until bedtime. She stayed awake for a long time, thinking about Benedict with hopeless misery; falling in love with him had certainly complicated matters, especially as he had shown no inclination to do the same with her. Now the chance that he would really even feel a fondness for her was so remote as to be laughable. She did her best to cheer herself up with the reflection that they hadn't been married long. There were years ahead of them, surely in time they could achieve some kind of . . . what was it that he had said? Harmony?

It was most fortunate that Joanne should ring the following morning and insist on them going to dinner with Everard. 'Of course, I'll be there,' she chuckled. 'We're going to talk about getting married, isn't it thrilling?' And when Prudence had accepted: 'You heard about Myra? Good riddance, I say. She, was set on getting Benedict for herself ever since his first wife died; not that he ever encouraged her to imagine she might be in the running.' She didn't wait for Prudence to reply. 'See you both this evening, then— dinner will be at eight o'clock, let us know if Benedict's going to be held up.'

Prudence told him at lunch and he agreed placidly. 'I should be home as usual for tea,' he told her. 'Are you doing anything special this afternoon?'

She shook her head. 'We'll go for a walk with Henry and then I'll take Sibella into town to get her a few things she'll need before we go to England.'

'Walk to the shops, then meet me at the hospital at four o'clock—we'll see what we can find for her to give Granny Trent and Aunt Nancy.'

Something Dutch, Sibella had insisted, so after deliberation, they bought a set of coffee spoons in silver, and Delft china, a blue bon-bon dish on a silver stand. To these Sibella, with her own pocket money, purchased a hideously gay tea-cloth and a tin of *hopjes*, a kind of hard toffee. She had a few gulden over, so she bought a packet of highly coloured sweets which she gave to Prudence with the instructions that they were to be shared fairly between her and Papa. It was a happy little interlude, and Prudence reflected sorrowfully that that was how it should be each and every day.

She changed into a calf-length dark green velvet skirt and a cream chiffon blouse for Everard's dinner party. Casting a critical eye over her reflection when she was ready, she conceded that she looked nice. She caught up an angora wrap and ran downstairs, rather on the late side, to find Benedict waiting with no sign of impatience in the hall.

The drive there was so short that there was no need to talk, and once in Everard's house, Joanne took the conversation into her own hands, talking non-stop about their plans, what she intended to do with the house, where they would go for their honeymoon. She laughed apologetically. 'I'm so full of me,' she said. 'It's like being in a lovely dream, I'm terrified that I'll wake up, and then I look at Everard and know that it's for real.' She beamed at Prudence. 'Isn't it a marvellous feeling, knowing that you're loved without reservations?'

'Oh, yes, marvellous,' agreed Prudence. 'It's all so exciting.' She looked at Everard. 'Do you mind your house being entirely made over?'

He laughed. 'Not in the least. I had no idea I was so interested in carpets and curtains until Joanne took me in hand!'

They all laughed over their drinks, and presently went in to dinner and later sat round the fire, the two women engrossed in wedding clothes, the men deep in a discussion about a new type of anaesthetic machine.

Joanne, pausing in the middle of a serious discussion about her wedding hat, said: 'Listen to them—they sound like a couple of old bachelors!'

Everard gave her a loving look. 'But, darling, until very recently we both were.'

'Well, it's a good thing we came along when we did. You're going to change your life style. I've every intention of having at least one baby, and I'm certain Prudence will have dozens . . .'

Benedict laughed: 'Dozens? My dear Joanne, I'm a busy man as it is!'

Prudence joined in the laughter because if she hadn't they would have noticed. Actually she felt more like crying.

The next few days went quickly enough. She packed for the three of them, checked her passport and money, had a long session with Sitska, gave Ork careful instructions about Henry, who was already looking gloomy at the sight of the luggage, and had coffee with various ladies whose invitations she had accepted. What with these activities, besides Sibella to play with and the odd letter to type, she was kept busy enough, so that when Benedict was home there were plenty of mundane things to talk about. He for his part, since they would be away for ten days or so, had a full day at his consulting rooms and quite often brought work home with him; notes to be written up, notes to colleagues about shared patients, notes to his registrar. He worked steadily until late at night, apologising to her for leaving her alone so much. His manner was friendly, but she sensed a withdrawal, although she found it impossible to tell if he were angry or hurt or just not interested. She forbore from questioning him about the trip to England. She knew where they were to go, but he had not told her anything about their schedule. She supposed she would be left to her own devices while he was lecturing and possibly accompany him to any social events that had been planned. She was determined to put on a brave face and act the happy wife. Presumably she was expected to be. Beyond that she wasn't prepared to think, not for the moment at any rate.

They were to go via the Hoek of Holland to Harwich and take the Aston Martin, since that would be the easiest way for Sibella, and it also meant that Benedict could do a full day's work before they needed to leave for the night boat. Prudence spent the day keeping an excited little girl as calm as possible, and taking Henry for an extra walk to make up for their absence. They had dinner early with Sibella, loaded up the car and set off. Now that they were actually on their way, Prudence felt a thrill of excitement. Perhaps there would be the opportunity to have a talk with Benedict, not just the polite talk they had been exchanging for the last week or so, but a real honest talk about the two of them. She wasn't going to tell him that she loved him, but perhaps she could let him see that she would like to start again, get back on to their old friendly footing. It struck her that the feeling of instant liking which they had had for each other when they first met, instead of blossoming into something deeper had dwindled away.

Of course there was no chance to say anything on the journey, Sibella talked non-stop and needed her questions answered, and once they were on board and Prudence had put the little girl to bed, Benedict, over a drink in the bar, suggested mildly that she might like to go to bed too.

She would have to be patient and pick the right moment, she decided as she got into the narrow bed beside Sibella's.

CHAPTER NINE

ENGLAND, in the dim light of early morning and with a faint drizzle falling, was hardly welcoming. Sibella, standing between Prudence and Benedict at the rails, watching the ferry berth, remarked in a disappointed voice that it looked exactly like Holland.

'And that's a good thing,' observed Benedict matter-of-factly, 'because you'll feel at home here, won't you?'

Prudence squeezed the small gloved hand. 'You liked Aunt Nancy at the wedding, didn't you?'

'Yes, but I like you better. Will you be gone for many days?'

'No, love, and you'll have such fun you won't find it a long while.'

They went down to the car presently, and since the ferry was half empty they were on their way within half an hour. Benedict drove steadily for half an hour and then slowed as they reached a small village and stopped before an old gabled hotel fronting the main street. 'Breakfast,' he said, 'is a meal I cannot do without. Let's see what we can get.'

They had a table in the small dining room, at a bow window overlooking the street, and since they had had only tea and biscuits when they had been called on board, they ate with healthy appetites. They went on again presently, joining the thickening stream of traffic, and since the journey from Harwich was under eighty miles, they were threading their way through the London suburbs by mid-morning.

Prudence hadn't bothered to find out much about Benedict's flat in London. She had asked where it was and had been told that it was a small place close to Wigmore Street. Her knowledge of London was largely confined to the shopping streets and Nancy's flat, but she had guessed vaguely that it would be somewhere to the west of the city. The early morning rush hour was well over and the lunch time traffic hadn't started; they went comparatively easily across the city and presently turned away from the crowded main streets to the contrasting quiet of the elegant side streets. Benedict drove up one of these and then turned off into a tree-lined cul-de-sac lined with tall Regency houses. He pulled up before one of these. 'Well, here we are,' he observed. 'The flat's on the second floor.' Prudence and Sibella got out and gazed around them; it was remarkably peaceful and quiet and she said in some surprise: 'It's peaceful!'

She took Sibella's hand and followed him across the narrow pavement and in through the front door. The small lobby opened out into a much larger hall with a staircase at one side. 'No lift,' said Benedict. 'If I want to see patients here I borrow a room on the ground floor—they're rented out to medical men.' They reached a landing and went up on to the next floor. The landing here was small with only one door. Benedict opened it with a key and held the door open for them to go through. The flat was surprisingly roomy, with a comfortable sitting room, a small dining room, a compact kitchen and three bedrooms as well as a bathroom and a shower. The third bedroom was very small indeed, but the furniture had been well chosen to give as much space as possible. Sibella instantly claimed it for her own and Prudence, ushered into the room next to it, was delighted to find that it overlooked a minute courtyard at the back of the house. There wasn't much to see, but the wall around it was covered with Virginia Creeper, glowing red and yellow, and there were chrysanthemums in the small centre bed.

Benedict went back to the car to collect the luggage and she peeped into the other bedroom and then into the sitting room. 'It's all very clean and tidy,' she observed when he came back.

'Someone comes in regularly; she'll be here in the morning. I had thought we might all go out to lunch and perhaps you wouldn't mind getting a meal this evening. The fridge should be well stocked.'

'I'd love to; it's the most super little kitchen. Do you have to lecture or anything today?'

He smiled a little. 'No—tomorrow morning at eleven o'clock. I must make some phone calls today, though. Call Nancy and your mother if you would like to. I'll make some coffee while you settle Sibella.'

When they had had their coffee he spent some time on the phone. He seemed to know a great many people rather well, Prudence decided, trying not to listen while she unpacked the things they would want for their two days' stay in London. It was well after midday by the time he had finished and they walked the short distance to Ici Paris, a charming little restaurant where it seemed Benedict was in the habit of eating when he was in London, and since the rest of the day was theirs in which to do what they wished, they strolled along Oxford Street and then into New Bond Street and down the Burlington Arcade, where

Benedict bought Sibella a shockingly expensive dress, and then, because Prudence had admired it, a cashmere sweater in exactly the right shade of green to go with her hair.

They had tea presently and then took a taxi back to the flat, where Prudence, very much on her mettle, retired to the kitchen, leaving father and daughter to amuse each other, while she saw to the supper.

The meal was pronounced a great success, although, as she modestly averred, the success was largely due to the lavish contents of the fridge. Sibella went to bed as soon as the meal was over, and when Prudence went back to the sitting room it was to find Benedict sitting at a desk between the narrow windows, surrounded by papers. She offered help in a hesitant manner and felt inordinately hurt when he said no abruptly, so that she said at once: 'Then I'll go to bed too—it's been quite a day. I've left coffee on the stove for you. Will breakfast at half past eight do?'

He looked up briefly. 'Yes, thanks. Goodnight, Prudence.'

She didn't go to sleep at once, and when she did, it was a heavy slumber from which she was roused in the morning by Benedict with morning tea.

She shot up in bed, her hair a burnished tangle. His 'good morning' was casual, but he added: 'You look like the Sleeping Beauty in that blue silk nightie with your hair all over the pillow.' He put a cup and saucer down on the bedside table. 'Sibella's awake; she wants to get into your bed.'

'She does most mornings, just for a few minutes.' Prudence tried to keep her voice as matter-of-fact as his while she savoured being a Sleeping Beauty even if he hadn't meant it. Sibella came prancing in then, and

Benedict fetched his own cup and sat on the end of the bed while they discussed what they should do with the day. 'You have to count me out until about five o'clock' he reminded them. 'How about the Zoo or the Tower?'

They decided on the Tower of London in the morning and after lunch another visit to the shops. 'Take a taxi to Harrods and spend the afternoon there,' suggested Benedict, 'and take a taxi back here. I'll let you have a key. You'll be all right?'

They had a lovely day. Sibella was taken round-eyed round the Tower, given lunch at a quiet little restaurant nearby and then transported to Harrods, where the pair of them spent a blissful afternoon. As Prudence explained afterwards, they hadn't really needed to buy anything, but an extra lipstick was always useful to have, so were angora gloves for Sibella and a silk scarf for herself, and they spent a great deal of time finding a present for Benedict. Sibella chose a bright yellow ballpoint pen with his initial stuck on its top and paid for it with her own pocket money from the little bag Prudence had given her. 'You must buy Papa a present too,' she insisted, so they spent another twenty minutes or so looking at everything on display in the men's department until finally Prudence decided on a small calf-bound pocketbook. Probably he would never use it, but she would not upset Sibella by buying nothing at all. They had tea before they went back to the flat—tiny sandwiches and tea-cakes and rich creamy confections, and the little girl was pink-cheeked with delight. 'I only wish Papa was here,' she confided to Prudence.

Prudence squeezed a small hand. 'So do I, darling, but we'll see him this evening.'

He was there waiting for them when they got back, ready to ask Sibella all the right questions about her day and toss her in the air and declare that he'd never had such a splendid pen in his life before and he'd use it every day.

'Mama's got a present too,' said Sibella, so that she had to hand over the pocketbook.

'Just what I wanted, my dear. Now I can write in it with my new pen.'

He had a lecture to give the next day too, but not until the afternoon. 'I'll drive you over to Nancy's and collect you when I'm through,' he told Prudence.

'I'm not coming back here? You want me to take everything with me?'

He nodded. 'Why not? I'm due in Birmingham tomorrow—we can drive up that evening. We shall be staying with the Senior Medical Consultant and his wife—I've met them both, they're a charming couple. I lecture there in the morning and we can leave after lunch; it's less than ninety miles to Bristol, and we'll be there for two days.'

'Oh, will we?' asked Prudence faintly. 'And then where do we go?'

'Edinburgh, two days there, and then Liverpool only one day, back to Oxford for another two days and then a couple of days with your people.' He added: 'Of course, if you find it too boring or tiring, you can go to Little Amwell whenever you wish.'

The haste with which she answered brought a gleam to his eye. 'Oh, no—I'm sure I shall enjoy it enormously.'

They had a rapturous welcome from Nancy. 'James is coming home early, he'd hate to miss you. We're so excited about having Sibella to stay.' She bent to hug the little girl. 'We'll have such fun, and we'll go to your granny's house and be waiting for Mummy and Daddy when they get home.'

They had lunch together before Benedict went back to give his lecture.

'He must be a clever devil,' commented Nancy, 'rushing round giving lectures off the cuff with hardly a pause. What does he lecture about, for heaven's sake?'

To which Prudence had to reply that she wasn't quite sure. Nancy gave her an old-fashioned look. 'Ah, well, you'll have nice long stretches together in the car.'

The men arrived within ten minutes of each other and there was ample time for tea before Benedict said: 'Well, we'd better be on our way. It'll take a couple of hours and the Slaters expect us for dinner.'

He picked up Sibella and gave her a kiss and put a small box into her hand. 'You may open that when we've gone, love, Aunt Nancy will help you with it. It'll help pass the time.'

'What did you give her?' asked Prudence as they drove away.

'A watch. One of those gaudy red things children love.' He glanced at her. 'She'll be all right. James tells me they've got something planned for every single day.'

They drove in silence for a little while, then once on the M1 he sent the car up to a steady seventy. 'The Slaters live just outside central Birmingham— Edgbaston. I'll be driving in with Tom Slater in the morning and I'll have lunch at the hospital. You'll like Margaret, I think. There'll be a few people there this evening, by the way. We shall leave tomorrow afternoon for Bristol. We are to stay at the Grand Hotel, and I lecture at the University there, I also have to go to the children's hospital after lunch. You'll be all right on your own? I should be back by tea time.'

'Perfectly all right, thank you.' She was dying to ask him why he had wanted her to come with him. He told her without the need of questions, though.

'This is the first time that we have been alone since we married, Prudence, and it seemed to me that it was high time that we had a little time to ourselves.'

A little time was right, considering the schedule he had just outlined.

'Why?' she asked blandly.

He went on as though she hadn't spoken. 'We have to talk—about us. In the meantime shall we just enjoy ourselves as much as possible?'

She said 'yes' in a rather bewildered voice, and since half a loaf was better than no bread at all, closed her mind to her many problems and said again quite urgently: 'Oh, yes, let's!'

The Slaters lived in a large, awkward Edwardian villa with a nice garden. It was furnished in comfort and in rather an old-fashioned style, but since it was obvious that they were perfectly happy in it and happy with each other, that was unimportant. They welcomed Prudence and Benedict with a kindly warmth which swept them indoors to the fire, to sit for a few minutes before Mrs Slater led Prudence upstairs. 'Dinner's at half past eight, so you've got more than half an hour, my dear. You're in here,' she opened a door on to a large bedroom furnished with light oak furniture, out of date but beautifully polished. 'And I made up a bed in the dressing room for Benedict; he explained that he'd have to work on his next lecture and didn't want to disturb you. Come down when you're ready.'

There were several people for dinner. Prudence, shaking hands and exchanging civilities, hoped silently that she would pass muster as an eminent physician's wife. As a matter of fact, she did more than that. Her looks alone caught everyone's eye, and she had chosen to wear a misty grey silk dress, rather demure and frightfully expensive, which did wonders for her hair. The evening passed pleasantly enough and so, for that matter, did the next morning, gossiping with Mrs Slater. Friends came in for lunch and before she knew where she was Benedict was there again, suggesting placidly that they should leave.

Driving down to Bristol, she asked if the lecture had gone well.

'I think so—I hope so. At any rate, I remembered to say all the things I wanted to say and I had none of those awful blank moments when one can't remember what one is talking about.'

Prudence enjoyed every minute of the ninety-mile journey; they seemed to have slipped back into their first easy friendship and talking was easy. It was a pity that they were able to go the whole way down the motorway, for they were in Bristol far more quickly than she could have wished, but she cheered up when she discovered that they would have the evening together at the hotel. She changed into something pretty for dinner and went down to join Benedict in the bar.

There were two men with him; elderly, pleasant and self-assured. Benedict introduced them as Professor Black and Dr Coles, both from the Royal Infirmary, who had been kind enough to come along and make sure that they were comfortable.

They beamed at her, plied her with sherry and then stayed and had dinner with them, and after that meal, over coffee in the lounge, they began a discussion about blood groups, so that presently Prudence wished them a gracefully worded goodnight and went to her room. And when, she thought forlornly, was there going to be any time to talk?

Certainly not in Bristol. She barely glimpsed Benedict all day and when he did return at last he brought with him Professor Black, this time accompanied by his wife. Prudence, saying all the right things, and looking delighted to see them, sat through a long-drawn-out dinner, exchanging nothings with Mrs Black while she held back frustrated rage.

It was a long drive to Edinburgh; they left after breakfast and drove endlessly north. 'Three hundred and sixty-five miles to go,' Benedict had told her casually as they got into the car. 'Say six hours driving, allowing for hold-ups, another hour and a half to eat. We should be thereby early evening.'

'And where do we stay?'

'Ah, yes—with Professor MacKin and his wife—two days, four lectures.' He turned to smile at her. 'Enjoying yourself?'

'Enormously,' she had said valiantly. 'I phoned Sibella yesterday, she sent her love.'

'We must find her a present, mustn't we? That was a pretty grey dress you wore at the Slaters'. You're making an impression, Prudence.'

She went a pleased pink. 'Oh, thank you; I'm trying my best . . .'

He said placidly: 'You don't have to try very hard to have the men buzzing round you like flies.'

She drew a quick breath. 'And would you mind?'

'You asked me that question once before, do you remember? My answer is the same.' He slowed the car. 'I'm going to turn off here; there's a pub somewhere near here where we can lunch.'

He had the most irritating way of preventing her from asking questions. She would have liked to have continued reminiscing about Nancy's wedding and their first meeting, but it was evident that she wasn't going to be given the chance. Never mind, she consoled herself, there were several days left. She counted them silently. Surely there would be a chance for them to talk—really talk about themselves; in the meantime it was heaven just to be with him.

There was no chance. She hardly saw him in Edinburgh and when they were together there were other people there—a small evening reception when she barely spoke to him for the whole evening; a lunch party when he was at the other end of the table. Edinburgh proved disappointing, and so did Liverpool, and she could have wept with vexation as they drove towards Oxford. Two days more and they would be at Little Amwell. And although they had travelled all those miles together, never once had they talked about anything other than his work, the cities they had visited and the people they had met. They were as far apart as ever.

They were to stay with an old acquaintance of Benedict's, one of the consultants at the hospital where Benedict was due to lecture, and as they reached the outskirts of Oxford Prudence said suddenly: 'I should like to come to your lecture—one of them, at any rate.'

'Are you interested in polycythaemia?' Benedict sounded mildly amused.

'I haven't the least idea what it might be,' observed Prudence coolly, 'but I should like to attend one of your lectures.'

'There's no reason why you shouldn't.' He was casually helpful. 'I'll take you along with me tomorrow, though I'm afraid you'll be bored.'

She refrained from telling him that nothing he did or said would ever bore her. She thanked him, adding: 'And you don't have to bother about me afterwards. I can go shopping or something or take a taxi.'

'We can talk about that later. Here we are.'

Dr Cruickshank was a good deal older than Benedict, and his wife, a round cosy little woman, treated Prudence as though she had been one of her teenage daughters. When Benedict explained later about Prudence going to a lecture, she said at once: 'Oh, that's nice, you'll enjoy that, my dear. Benedict will be able to arrange for someone to bring you back here for lunch. He'll be going to the consultants' room for his, I expect. And you won't be missing anything; they drink pints of beer and talk about the most revolting things!'

Prudence laughed: 'Then I'm glad I'm not invited. But I'm sure I can find my way back here . . .'

'I'm sure you can too, Prudence, but I'll get someone to bring you back.' Benedict spoke casually, but she didn't argue. He seldom raised his voice and at times one would imagine him to be easygoing in the extreme, but she had learned that he liked things to be done his way once he'd made up his mind.

There were, inevitably, people coming in for drinks. Prudence went upstairs presently to change in the comfortable bedroom with its surprisingly modern bathroom and the dressing room beyond. 'Very

considerate of Benedict to sleep there,' Mrs
Cruickshank had commented, and meant it. 'I expect
he sits up until all hours when he's got a lecture to put
together. It must be quite hard work.'

The evening was pleasant and Prudence, in the grey
dress, made a hit with the guests. It wasn't that she
was just pretty; she was a good listener, never tried to
attract attention, and was as happy talking to some
crusty old professor as someone of her own age.

They were to leave the next day, after Benedict had
given another lecture in the morning and she had had
an early lunch at the Cruickshanks. She didn't see him
to speak to for more than a few moments until they
were in the car driving out of Oxford. True, she had
attended the lecture, and sat bursting with pride while
he talked, not understanding a word of it.

'Well, that's over,' observed Benedict. 'I've left a
trail of envious men behind me—not because of my
lectures, but because of my beautiful and charming
wife.'

Prudence digested this with pleasure and then
frowned. 'Is that why I came with you? To see if I was
suitable to be the wife of an eminent doctor?'

They had stopped waiting for the traffic lights to
change. He turned to look at her. He said silkily: 'It's
high time we had our talk, my dear.'

'More than time,' she snapped back, 'but you've left
it a bit late.'

'Never too late.' The lights changed and he drove
on, and she didn't say more, for the traffic was heavy,
but presently she exclaimed: 'We're not going south—
you're on the Warwick road!'

'That's right. That's where we are going.'

'Another lecture?' she ventured, puzzled.

'I hope not.' And when she glanced sideways at him, his profile looked so stern she decided not to say anything more for the moment.

He drove fast up the A423, through Banbury and then on again until Southam, when he took the road to Warwick.

'Warwick?' queried Prudence at a complete loss.

His, 'Yes, my dear,' offered no clue.

They drove through Warwick and out on to the Stratford-upon-Avon road, but before they reached the outskirts of the town he turned sharply through big open gates and went slowly uphill between tall trees. 'Warwick Castle?' asked Prudence. 'Why have we come here? They close in two hours—it said so at the gate.'

'Two hours can be a long time, and we've come here because it should be quiet—I mean peacefully quiet.' He gave her a quick smile. 'Here's the car park.'

The man in charge was friendly. 'Almost no visitors,' he told them. 'You'll have the place to yourselves—we close at five o'clock, mind.'

They walked up the rest of the drive and through the barbican. The castle was built round a rough circle of grass and the car attendant had been quite right. It was so quiet, if Prudence had had a pin handy, she would have heard it drop.

'Not the dungeons,' said Benedict, and took her arm. 'Let's try the Private Apartments.'

They went through a wide door at the top of stone steps and stepped into another world. Two ladies were chatting just inside the door, but beyond wishing them good day, they left them to their own devices.

There was a lot to see—music room, library, boudoir, drawing room ... Prudence, interested despite herself, spoke her thoughts. 'I wonder if they were happy?' She gestured to the figures in their elegant, elaborate clothes, sitting in apparent conversation while powdered footmen poured tea.

'Happy? If happiness means great wealth, a great many servants at one's beck and call, cupboards full of clothes and magnificent jewels, probably they were happy.'

They had paused and were standing at a window which overlooked a magnificent waterfall below them. She felt Benedict's arm round her shoulders and trembled a little. 'Happiness for me is loving someone so deeply that they're part of life, so dear that there's no living without them.' He turned her round and held her tight. 'That's how I feel about you, my darling.'

Prudence sniffed into the tweed of his jacket. 'Just now? Just this instant?' she asked, and felt him laugh.

'Oh, my dearest, I've been in love with you since I turned round at Nancy's wedding and saw you just behind me.'

'You could have said so.' Her voice came muffled.

'And you would have shied away like an ill-used little animal, afraid to be hurt again.'

He put a hand under her chin so that she had to look up at him. 'I thought—rightly or wrongly, I don't know—that if I left you alone, treated you as a friend, you would in time come to love me too.'

Prudence gave a small choking sob. 'I've been in love with you for weeks and weeks.' She added for no reason at all: 'That beastly Myra and you being horrid about Everard . . . you encouraged me!'

'I felt I ought to do so. And my darling girl, can you not forget Myra? She never meant anything, you know.' He smiled slowly. 'As to that, what about beastly Tony?'

She chuckled on a sob. 'What a waste of time!' she said.

'Well now, we'll start making up for that this minute.' His arms tightened so that she could scarcely breathe. He kissed her gently at first and then quite roughly, and one of the ladies, coming softly to make sure that they weren't stealing anything, stood and watched, her mouth open. She was a sentimental little lady, with old-fashioned ideas about love; these two elegant people standing there with eyes for no one but each other were exactly as she imagined love might be, given the right man and woman. She sighed and slipped down the stairs again and told her companion, who in her turn went to have a look. When she got back she said: 'We close in an hour. Ought we to—well, remind them?'

She went back once more and found them standing very close together at the window. Rather at a loss, she observed: 'The castle is most interesting, isn't it? There's a tea-room in the cellars, if you would care for a cup—we shut quite soon.'

'My wife and I find everything quite . . .' Benedict paused, 'wonderful, and we'd like tea before we go.'

'Down this passage and through the door at the bottom of the stairs.'

She watched them go and hurried back to her friend. 'Just fancy, they're married!' she observed. 'I didn't think they would be, they looked so in love.' She sighed. 'She was so pretty too.'

Prudence and Benedict wandered arm in arm along the passage and down the stairs. At the bottom he took her in his arms again and kissed her. 'We'll be a little late back. I'll phone your parents, Sibella could stay up for once, couldn't she? We're not far from the M5, we can have a quick run to just below Bristol and cut across through Glastonbury.'

'I don't mind where we go or what we do,' said Prudence, 'as long as I'm with you.' She added: 'And the children of course.'

He kissed her again. 'Of course,' he agreed. 'All ten of them.' He took her arm. 'Let us have tea, my dearest love.'

A WORD ABOUT THE AUTHOR

Betty Neels, whose first Harlequin was published in 1970, is well-known for her stories set in the Netherlands. This is not surprising. Betty is married to a Dutchman, and she spent the first twelve years of her marriage in Holland. Today she and her husband, Johannes, return there as often as three times a year.

As Betty travels, always visiting some fresh spot in Holland, she chooses houses, streets and villages to use in her books; whenever possible she will venture inside privately owned buildings. "And of course," she laughs, "I tend to go through life eavesdropping on conversations in buses and trains and shops." An excellent way, we think, to garner ideas for romance novels.

Betty Neels is a retired nurse. Today she and Johannes make their home in a small three-hundred-year-old stone cottage in England's West Country, where, she says, life moves along at a pleasantly unhurried pace.